The Namaste Club

A Novel

Tim Gurung

tara
India Research Press

tara
India Research Press
Flat. 6, Khan Market, New Delhi - 110 003
Ph: 24694610; Fax: 24618637
www.indiaresearchpress.com
contact@indiaresearchpress.com

2022

ISBN 13: 978-81-8386-197-7

Printed and Bound in India

*This book is dedicated to
our very own Nepalese community
in Hong Kong and the Nepalese diaspora
living around the globe.*

Chapter 1

The old and unattractive twelve-story building stood in the middle of crowded streets in the Jordan Market area. The creamy paint on the building walls was peeling off in many places. Wherever there was a patch of paint, there were doodles with bad graffiti on it. Evidently, the building hadn't seen a new stroke of fresh paint for ages. All the apartments had doors with a metal grille, and most of them were old and rusted. The entire building was occupied by low-income families from rural backgrounds. Everyone had to use the stairs for everything, making the lives of those living on the upper floors quite miserable. Unlike other buildings in the city, the main entrance to this building was always kept open without any monitoring or security; anyone could come in or go out of the building at any time. Most of the apartments, especially on the lower floors, were rented out cheaply and used to store illegal goods, hold meetings, indulge in some gambling, pimping and so on.

All the buildings in the vicinity were of a similar height except for a few in new and bigger shopping malls. The sidewalk was bordered with small and medium-sized shops, and the street was always crowded with people and cars. Any leftover space was snapped up by huddling hawkers, and everyone seemed busy and intent on something as if it were the last chance of their lives. The market remained open until very late at night.

Just like the main entrance of the building, the staircase to the rooftop always remained open, and everyone who wanted could venture there. Most of the old buildings in Hong Kong have illegal structures on their rooftops, and this particular temporary building was no different. It was built with metal sheets and equally divided into six rooms. Each pair of rooms had a separate door. Most of the rooms were padlocked and used for storage purposes. A group of four men, about fifty years old, who spoke the same language and were very good friends, would meet weekly in the two rooms the farthest from the staircase.

The men would probably be considered a weird bunch. They would gather there on Saturday afternoons and go home late Saturday night. They wouldn't appear until the following Saturday, always at the same time. It was a ritual that had been consistently going on for years. Not once did they fail to appear at the usual time, which was quite an achievement.

The inside of their special place was quite plain and humdrum, not much was significant or noticeable, and most of it was almost empty. The entire floor was covered with wood-veneer-printed plastic mats. There was an elevated cooking area built of bricks in the right-hand corner from the entrance, and next to it was a water tap and sink. A blue gas cylinder was placed underneath the cooking area and a large metal wok was permanently placed on the stove. Between the stove and the sink, there was an area, almost two-feet-long, used to store necessary groceries and utensils. The whole place was almost two hundred square feet in area, but without any furniture. Only a few mattresses, cushions, pillows, blankets and some towels were stored on the opposite side of the stove. Although it had been some kind of secret meeting place for them, where they could come and find solace and peace, it was a very simple, quiet and primitive-looking place, and it had remained so for a very long time.

Their hideaway was nicely hidden from the glitter and hustle-bustle of city life. It was no example of modern sophistication or civility, it represented a primitive way of living, yet one that didn't diminish its value or significance to its occupants and served the same purpose as other fancy and reputable places do for opulent and powerful people. Both rich and poor need a place to go where they can relax, find peace and be happy.

Even though the mysterious group came from different ethnicities, those belonging to the group spoke the same language. They were not only attentive, respectful and convivial but also cared for each other. It was not just a friendly, but also a brotherly union. They were always available for each other as comrades-in-arms.

The friendship was purely based on trust, respect and mutual affinity; it was not spoiled by the social structural system of hierarchy and stature, and it totally operated on equilibrium. They had neither leader nor follower; all had the same right, and status within the group. All the necessary decisions concerning the group were made collectively as a whole. Whenever there was an issue, it was thrashed out between the four, and decisions were only taken and steps implemented when all four were in agreement. It was the unity, the habit of playing by the rules, and mutual respect between the four that had made the group last for so long.

Hong Kong is a rich, vibrant and sophisticated place, there is no shortage of popular clubs and they certainly come in different sizes and shapes – not to mention the prestige that comes with the highly inflated egos of its affluent members. There was the HK Jockey Club, the American Club, the Foreign Correspondents Club, the Fan Ling Golf Club, the Hong Kong Club, the HK Country Club, and so on. But for the four men, the Namaste Club was what they could call their own.

The quiet, remote and primitive set-up on the roof of the old building in the middle of Jordan market was a typical example of people's ingenuity and improvisation, that it was lacking in grandiosity and luxury didn't make it less significant than the other so-called-big clubs from the mega city. It somehow managed to serve the same purpose for its members as the other big and famous clubhouses did in their own respect. It was not only the place where they met each Saturday evening, spent quality resting time and found solitude, but also formed a team of brothers-in-arms and made important decisions of their lives here. They were very fond of the place.

This story is about the Namaste Club, how it began, the important role it played in the lives of its four members and their respective families, and the remarkable changes it brought about in their lives. For others, it was nothing more than an abandoned place with not much value. But for them, it was a place they could call their own, and most importantly, it was their lifeline.

Chapter 2

Always properly dressed, he was five-feet-eight-inches tall with a slim body, a swarthy complexion, and nicely trimmed short black hair. Black eyes and an unusually large nose dominated his round weathered face. He was a cultured man, well organized and disciplined and, most noticeably, he was a man of few words. Most of the time, he would remain quiet but attentive, and always waited for others to stop before he would start talking. It was not in his nature to be loud; he would never interrupt while the others were talking, and he was always polite to others. Although the group had no hierarchical system, he happened to be the most liked and respected member of the group and was discretely known as its brains. All the events that took place within the group were mostly his ideas; they would discuss it in great detail and put them into practice only when all four members had unanimously supported it. His name was Ram Bahadur Gurung, and he was an ex-Gurkha soldier who hailed from Pokhara, Nepal. He worked as a security guard at the nearby shopping mall, and lived on the same street with his wife and two sons.

Another member was almost five-foot-seven with a strong and bulky body and scruffy long black hair mixed with grey. He had a rather fair complexion and was always dressed in blue jeans, a t-shirt and hiking boots. His round face with lively brown eyes, which were usually bright and cheerful, always sported a broad smile. He was loud, strong and laughed a lot at small incidents.

He not only talked a lot but also had a bad habit of cracking cheap jokes and mostly ended up laughing at his own expense. He was a carefree person with a pure heart that never harboured any ill feelings toward another human being. Sher Bikram Thapa, an ex-Gurkha soldier hailed from Baglung, Western Nepal. He was a nice guy and always ready to help, and contributed to the group through his will and strength. He was rightly known as the muscle of the group and was currently living in Yuen Long, the New Territories of Hong Kong with his wife and two daughters. He worked in the construction industry.

Krishna Sharma, a well-educated civilian from Kathmandu, Nepal, somehow ended up in Hong Kong without plausible explanation, and he ran a grocery store on a nearby street, which was close to where he lived with his wife, two sons and two daughters. He was more than six feet tall, very skinny and with long hands that could touch the ceiling without having to use a ladder. His long brown-complexioned face was hairy, dominated by black eyes and framed by long, curly black hair. He was always dressed in a collared shirt, long pants and sandals. Krishna was the most talkative one; he could spin a subject in many directions at one go, and he could keep on talking for hours without a break. He was appropriately known as the voice of the group, and he never failed to entertain them.

The fourth member of the group, Manohar Biswakarma (BK), was about five-foot-six with a plump body and a very handsome brown-complexioned face with innocent-looking black eyes. His face was framed by long and silky, curly black hair. He was a stylish guy and rather quiet. When he spoke, which was slowly, he had a nice, clear voice and when he finished talking, he'd smile infectiously. He was the youngest member, and because of his good nature and affable character, everybody liked him. He was undoubtedly the dearest of the whole group and aptly known as the prestige of the group. He was a fairly educated fellow with more inclination towards music than study, and hailed from

Eastern Nepal. He owned and ran his own restaurant in Hong Kong. He lived in Wan Chai with his wife, son and daughter.

This unusual bunch of people belonging to different ethnicities from Nepal, brought together by necessity rather than choice, had somehow managed to survive the test of time encumbered by social anomalies. They had come from such a different stratum of society that had they been in their own country, such a coming together of unusual people would have been almost unthinkable. But when you live in a foreign country, being from the same country can be enough to bring people closer. When you are in the disadvantageous position as a minority, every head counts and even people from far and away can become a close and trusted ally. Hong Kong is a very rich and developed place, almost 95 per cent of the locals are Chinese and the remaining population is made up of a few more ethnicities. Needless to say, just like many other big places in this world, it is the minority, who always end up doing the odd, dirty and poorly paid jobs that the locals don't want to touch. They all faced the same fate daily and mostly eked out a living by scraping through the bottom tiers of the job market, mostly as security guards, drivers, cleaners, domestic helpers, housekeepers, waiters, delivery boys and, sometimes, as owners of small eateries serving South Asian cuisines.

The weekly hideout was not only for a social gathering of like-minded members but also a place where they could talk freely. It was not only about family matters, hobbies and general affairs, but they also discussed serious issues they were facing in daily life and trying to find ways out as well. They could talk about almost anything; they had no-holds-barred discussions and everyone would pitch in to find a workable solution. The unconditional trust, camaraderie and respect between the four made it a very special place for all.

Each time they visited the place, they always returned with

a full backpack, with each one bringing different things. If one had drinks in his backpack, the others had food, snacks and other knick knacks. It was the sort of usual routine where everybody knew what to bring next without having to discuss it. If one brought drinks for the week, he would bring food the next week and snacks the next time and so on. It was a well-drilled rotation that had no repetition. They would come to their hideaway, eat, drink, and talk as they like, and behave like they were having the best times of their lives. They all remained together until the end, helped each other and shared their joys and sorrows as lifelong friends. It is the story of a rare and remarkable friendship.

Chapter 3

In the middle of Temple Street in Jordan Market, there was an old residential building that had no escalator, and most of the paintings on its walls were all chipped away. The ground floor of the building was used for shops as the other buildings nearby; the staircase was dark, damaged and littered with garbage. The building was not more than fifteen stories high, most of its outer facades were haphazardly laden with unscrupulous neon lights or signboards, and the remaining parts of the building housed illegal structures. Overall, it looked like an old, frail woman with dirty and frayed clothes carrying too much baggage around her enfeebled body and was waiting to collapse sometime soon. The place was noisy, crowded and most of the denizens living there were from low-income families. The first apartment right next to the staircase on the fourth floor was a typical Hong Kong flat with two small bedrooms, a small living room, a tiny kitchen and a bathroom. Due to a well-perceived superstition amongst the local Chinese community, this apartment carried another unspoken stigma. The word four and death sound the same in Cantonese. The locals commonly believe that 'four' brings bad luck and is inauspicious. As a result, no locals would take it willingly as their family residence, but cheap rent would attract mostly poor people for obvious reasons.

A double sofa made of vinyl was placed on one side of the front room with a coffee table and two metal folding stools on the opposite side. The third side of the room had a wooden display cabinet, while the other two sides were empty. Shelves of the display cabinets were filled with various decorative items and family photos, and there was a flat TV in the middle. The kitchen and the bathroom were on the fourth side of the apartment. The first separate room was just big enough for a double bed. The other room had a double bunk bed, a wooden study table and chair, and a pair of bean bags in an outrageously lurid green canvas. Most of the walls were empty except for a few hand drawings done by the children who slept there. The home had nothing unusual; it looked exactly like a normal, ordinary household. This was the Gurung family's home.

Ram Bahadur Gurung was a well-disciplined, cultured and honest man, and his peers liked and respected him for his sincerity. Ram is a very common and popular name, derived from one of the Hindu mythical Gods. This particular God is mostly revered for the manifestation of righteousness, duty and nobility. Bahadur, the middle name, means brave one and almost each and every boy born in that generation had it in their name. Gurung is the surname of hill people mostly from the midwestern part of Nepal, and it is one of the main ethnic groups of people from Western Nepal who were known to have joined the British Army contingent as Gurkhas. Almost each and every family of this particular group has some connection with the UK outfit one way or another. It is a very long and distinguished tradition continuing for more than two decades. Just like his fathers and uncles, he had joined the British Army as a Gurkha, served Her Majesty's Service with pride and honour for more than eighteen years as an Infantry Sergeant, and was eventually sent back to Nepal after his retirement. After spending all of his adult life abroad, he shared the same fate as all the other retired Gurkhas: he couldn't fit in the new society back in Nepal and was forced to find a way out as the others before him had.

When an opportunity to return to Hong Kong serendipitously appeared before him, he didn't think long before grabbing it, and came back again as a civilian. For the next few years, he struggled to find the right job and, just like most of the newcomers, he ended up doing all the odd and low-paying jobs that most of the locals didn't touch. His family joined him within a few years' time, but it took many hard and backbreaking years before they could eventually settle down in the new place, and finally feel as if they really belonged there. That move was almost twenty years before. The father of the Gurung family now worked as a security guard at the nearby shopping mall, and whatever the others might say, he genuinely believed in and called Hong Kong his home.

Ram Bahadur's wife, Gauri Maya Gurung, was a quiet, graceful and lively woman with a petite build. She was of fair complexion, and had a pair of vivid big eyes in a slim face. Her distinct look was heightened by long black silky hair always braided and adorned with colourful ribbons. Her sense of fashion was modest, not too bright, not too expensive, simple but elegant. She used to wear a simple pair of earrings, a gold-plated necklace, and a red tika (a traditional reddish/yellowish powder mark on the middle of the forehead). It was her inner strength, her adroitness in the kitchen and ability to keep the house in good order that helped keep the family as one. She would let Ram Bahadur take all the decisions at home. Although she never tried to take credit for anything, the mother of the Gurung family happened to be the family's main pillar. She not only worked miracles inside the home, but she also took on odd jobs from time to time and helped contribute to improving the financial condition of the family so that it did not fall into troubled times in a foreign place.

Ram Bahadur and Gauri had had an arranged marriage and they had two sons. Anmol (the precious one) Gurung was the first son of the Ram Bahadur Gurung family. He inherited most of his features from his father. He was a good, happy and respectful boy, but he wasn't very bright at school, yet he had never failed either, and to the relief of his overbearing parents, his growing up was pretty normal and trouble-free. He was the special one, hardly out of sight from his loving folks and their loving lives together. Despite failing to interact socially, communicating clearly and responding properly, he was still a very normal, active and lively boy, and his boyhood was spent in a happy environment.

His ongoing problems, which gradually became serious after his adolescence, restricted him from outside activities that a normal teenager would love to do, and before his eighteenth birthday, to the devastation of the Gurung family, his inherent problem had become so serious that he was no longer able to venture outside on his own, and was confined to the four walls of the house. He was diagnosed with severe Autistic Spectrum Disorder (ASD) and had to be taken care of by one of his parents all the time.

Trimol (three precious ones or trinity from Hindu mythology) Gurung was the younger son and had inherited his features and mental abilities from his mother's side. He was tall and had a skinny body frame, and he had enough steel to face the tough world alone by himself. Unlike his brother, he was blessed with a strong will, was extroverted and smart as well, and had excelled in multiple aspects of life. He was not only good at school but also good in making friends and was liked by all. There was a two-year age gap between the two brothers, but they looked almost the same age from very early on, and they were brought up like they were twins. Despite the same upbringing, they had completely contrasting characters and, in time became poles apart. As they grew older, the gap gradually grew wider. Anmol's ongoing health problem immensely upended his life.

Due to the unfavourable and solemn situation at home, Trimol learned to live an independent life from an early age and he found imaginative ways to make it an interesting and sustainable one. He was a quick learner; he had enough steel to survive on his own in this tough world. Parents tend to pay more attention to the weakest one amongst their offspring. By no means do they love their other children less, but they are just more worried about the troubled one. Since the Gurung family was no exception, he had to make a quick habit of self-sufficiency and protect himself from a very early age.

Before his eighteenth birthday, he understood the unavoidable situation at home and decided to face it like a brave man. He understood not only the importance of education in life, but also the actual situation in his not-so-affluent home. If he wanted to change that, he needed to land a decent job that paid well. He didn't want to end up like his father whose piffling pension was no use in an expensive city like Hong Kong, and he was determined to have at least a university degree to find himself a good job. He juggled half a dozen part-time jobs at a time when he was pursuing his university degree and, eventually, did not only graduate with flying colours but also landed a well-paid job in the banking industry within a month after graduation.

Unlike other outsiders who usually found Cantonese very hard to learn, he turned out to be very good at grasping it from the beginning and talked like a local without any difficulty whatsoever. The unexpected fluency in the local dialect gave him an unprecedented edge over his peers. He ended up marrying a local Chinese girl who had been his colleague at work for some time. The marriage created a lot of confusion and culture clashes at home, and for the sake of all the family members involved, it was eventually decided that they should find a place of their own and start living separately from the family. The Gurung household was already too small and congested for the expanded family, and the deteriorating health problems of the elder son also didn't help.

Living independently happened to be a very wise decision. They found their own place on the other side of Kowloon, which was a twenty-minute ride in the underground train, and they never failed to visit the parents over the weekends on a regular basis. Trimol was never more than a phone call away from his parents; he was always there for them and didn't shirk from his duty and obligation as a good son.

Chapter 4

Fifteen minutes away from the Yuen Long main train station, at walking distance, was a small community of about a dozen village houses, most of them two to three stories high. The houses were old, the roads were congested, and the place was full of dogs and cats. Most of the houses were occupied by the original owners: the indigenous village people of the New Territories. Since all of the young generations had already left for the main city, it was mostly the elders who were left behind to pick up the dirt around the village. Only on weekends or long public holidays did the youngsters return and make the village a lot noisier and livelier than usual.

Due to lack of space to live in a mega city like Hong Kong, people mostly chose to do so in tiny, congested places, and different floors in the same building or a house could be rented or sold separately. Households normally do rent out the extra spaces for additional income. A three-story village house can have three different families living on each floor, and usually the landlord occupies the main ground floor for easy access and control of the adjacent land around the house. Due to the open area on the rooftop, which can be used for many purposes, including drying clothes, the top floors were favoured by many and commanded better rents.

The first house at the village entrance was a three-story one.

The ground and second floors were occupied by the owner, and the top floor was rented to an outsider. The owners were an elderly couple who lived on the ground floor; the second floor was kept unrented, and mostly used by their children during weekends. The top floor had its own access through staircases from the outside. The open areas surrounding the main house were mostly used by the owners themselves. There were some plant holders, old bicycles, a granite table set with four chairs, and an open playing ground paved in stone.

All houses within the village had their own fenced-in yards with metal gates as a main entrance. Each house had their own worshipping place in the corner of this open area, and in the name of security, each household had at least two dogs of their own. As a result, whenever someone entered the village, it was always the dogs from the first house, whose main task was to raise an alarm. The other dogs followed suit, and in no time, everybody in the village knew what had happened. Since all the dogs were on leashes or locked inside the metal fences of those, the fear of being bitten by the dogs was remote, but it was the deterrence that they needed, and they had managed to do much more than that. Sometimes a display of force is mightier than a bite; for the fainthearted the threat was quite scary. The dogs had managed to keep the village trouble free by chasing away those potential petty thieves.

When someone entered the main entrance of the first house, there was a shoe rack on the left side and an open kitchen, and a seating area on the right side with a set of sofas and a coffee table. Attached to the wall of the seating area, there was a display rack with many shelves containing family photos, decorative objects and a big black flat-screen TV in the middle. The kitchen had two stoves, a refrigerator, two sinks, and a set of black plastic racks on the side filled with fresh vegetables and other grocery items. The kitchen and dining area were divided by a set of wooden display cabinets. The dining area was dominated by a large round wooden table with five chairs. Past the dining area were three bedrooms: two medium-sized rooms and one small one. The two bigger rooms each had a set of beds, a dressing table and a pair of cabinets for clothes, and the walls were covered with colourful posters, decorative objects and other vanity items. The small room was just big enough for a single bed. Clothes had to be stored in suitcases and pushed underneath the bed. All three rooms had one window each. The other side of those rooms had two separate bathrooms, and a small storage room. The way to the rooftop was from the outside, next to the main entrance. The open yard area was a very useful place for the family and used for almost everything from cleaning and drying clothes to eating and playing. It was also an ideal place for a nightly stroll under the open sky to breathe the fresh air and to have a peaceful moment.

Sher means lion, Bikram means valiant and Thapa was his surname. Sher Bikram Thapa was a loud, lively and affable man over fifty. He was an ex-Gurkha Army Corporal and had always worked in the construction industry since he moved to Hong Kong with his family after retirement. He was originally from Baglung, Western Nepal, served the British Gurkha Army for fifteen years and had made Hong Kong his permanent home since then. He had worked very hard in the backbreaking construction industry to raise his young family and hadn't had a single holiday hitherto in life. Thankfully, he was blessed with a strong body, a simple but optimistic character, and had a strong sense of responsibility. Working outside, in the rain, heat and storm, is already difficult, but working on tall buildings, underground tunnels, and in many other unfavourable conditions in the humid and unpredictable weather of Hong Kong is harder, and by the looks of it, he seems to have been made of real steel and sheer determination.

After contributing his good years to the British crown, he was dismissed to the backward hills of Western Nepal. The piffling pension from the British Raj would not have lasted that long back in Nepal. The skills he had learned in the army playing with the muzzle of a rifle wouldn't help much to boost his income so he could easily settle down with a comfortable life back in civilian society. It didn't take too long for him to realize his situation. His regimented lifestyle simply wouldn't fit into unruly civilian society, and he desperately needed a way out before he went insane. Luckily, his two daughters were born in Hong Kong before 1984, the year when the fate of tiny Hong Kong was agreed upon and sealed between the British and the Chinese. Children born before that cut-off date were eligible for the right of abode in Hong Kong. That fact eventually opened the door for his family to escape from the hardship of the hill people's life, and they were allowed to enter and settle in Hong Kong legally.

As the saying goes, the rest was history. Destiny had brought them back to Hong Kong, gave them a chance to settle down in a Yuen Long village and they had never left the place since then. The ever-smiling father of the Thapa family was a simple, honest and hardworking man, his habit of cracking cheap jokes making him a likable fellow amongst his peers. He no longer had the intention of ever vacating the village house as it reminded him of his old village back in Nepal.

Gita Thapa was a common name in Nepal. Just like most of the names in a religious society, it had something to do with the mythical Hindu scripture or goddess's name. She was a sporty woman, quite an able basketball player during her school years, and she was a born leader. During her husband's time in the army, she was so busy with the very demanding task of bringing up two daughters at the same time, she hardly had time to think about other things in life. All of her desires and hobbies in life had to take a backseat until the children were big enough to take care of themselves. Low-ranking soldiers in the army would normally get only one rare chance to bring their families to Hong Kong to spend their married lives. By chance, the Thapas had children of their own during that period, and they used to laugh a lot by calling themselves a baby-making factory. Once they had come back to Hong Kong and settled down, life was pretty hard and raising three girls at the same time was not that easy. Due to the difference in language, culture and the way of life between Hong Kong and Nepal, it was very difficult initially to earn a decent living and an almost never-ending struggle.

Hong Kong is an expensive place, especially for new migrants with limited or no skills. Most had to juggle with more than one regular job to just survive. The situation of the Thapa family was no different. Not only the father but also the mother had to seek out odd jobs such as waiting, cleaning and serving at an eatery and both parents worked really hard until their daughters were grown up. Once the children finished their studies, found decent jobs and started to bring more money home, Gita could finally take much-needed breaks and start thinking about her life again.

Rekha Thapa was a tall, attractive and dark-eyed young girl with fair skin. She had silky black curly hair, and an unwavering taste for exquisite things. Her fashion sense was very good. After finishing high school, she decided to find a job at a high-end beauty shop as an intern beautician, learning the trade along the way. She perfected her skills within a year before becoming a principal beautician with some loyal customers of her own. As she preferred to set a high standard and live by example, almost half of her salary was spent on her own vanity. She kept the other half for her own use. She would give whatever balance remained at the end to her mother as her contribution to the household. Her other personal skills included providing unsolicited advice to her younger sister on almost everything from ethics, relationships, personal hygiene, appearances, responsibilities and so on, and she tried hard to live by example. Before her twenty-eighth birthday, the eldest daughter of the Thapa family met a white guy from the United Kingdom who worked in insurance. Their marriage was celebrated with a lavish party at one of the high-end hotels in Hong Kong, and they started living in the city on their own. The eldest bird had flown the nest.

Disha Thapa was also a common name, and Disha literally means direction. The younger daughter of the Thapa family was a troubled child. She was not only carefree and fun-loving, she was less interested in school and indifferent as well as ignorant, and had a bad habit of waking up only after she had fallen off the cliff. She had a plump body from being a big eater, a large round face with swarthier skin and black short curly hair. Disha was always seen in casual jeans and a t-shirt. Unlike her big sister, she never cared about her appearance and make-up was the last thing on her mind, whether she was in the house or outside.

The simple task of finishing high school was a monumental hurdle, and she had to be virtually carried to the finish line by her two sisters throughout those years. The day she finally managed to complete high school, she celebrated it as if she were liberated from all the travails of life. Needless to say, the whole family was fully aware of her position, and the expectation bar for her was not set very high. When she somehow finished her studies, everyone was genuinely happy for her and relieved too. Then she started working at different jobs, sometimes she waited at a café or restaurant, at other times at hotels as a housekeeper, and she even tried being a shop assistant at various shops and boutiques. Whatever money she could get from those odd jobs, she would give to her mother and whenever she needed some money, she would take it from her mother. Most importantly, she didn't mind at all doing those odd jobs. She didn't give a damn about what the others thought or said about her, which helped make her a very happy, content and nice person at the same time. After working here and there for a few more years, she met a black guy, and despite the vehement opposition from the family, they got married eventually and started to live by themselves in a separate apartment in the city.

Chapter 5

Near the junction of Jordan Road and Temple Street, there was a small grocery shop, which stocked completely different products than other shops around it. It was less busy and not as crowded as its neighbours. It mostly sold goods imported from Nepal or India and almost all of the customers were from the local Nepalese community.

The entrance was simple and wide; it had neither glass doors nor display windows; instead it was fitted with a metal shutter that could be pulled up and down while opening and closing the shop. The inside of the shop was narrow with the centre of the floor kept empty as a passageway for customers. The side walls, fitted with wooden shelves, and part of the floors, were heavily laden with a variety of goods. Each shelf was full of packages and sacks full of rice, lentils, dried beans, instant noodles, potato, cabbage, cauliflower, onion, garlic, ginger, and more, and those heavy packages were placed along both walls and on the floor. At the back of the shop, there was a small counter, and the counter was filled with a cash register, a telephone, a small TV set, a notebook, a pen and a pencil, and many more handy things. Behind the counter was a black office chair, and the wall behind it also contained goods to sell. At the right-hand corner of that wall was an entrance that was covered by a shabby floral curtain.

Behind the curtain was the inner part of the shop, which

was the family living area and had a living room with colourful carpets on the floor, a sofa with a coffee table in front of it, a pair of open cabinets with shelves and a TV set. The walls had some family photos as well as religious pictures. Behind it was the family kitchen, behind the kitchen was the bathroom, and it had two bedrooms at the far end. The entire place was dark, and not very ventilated. This area worked as an underground burrow for the family.

Krishna Sharma (derived from the Hindu God's name) was a smart, talkative hardworking man who hailed from Kathmandu, Nepal's capital. From a very early age, he worked with an Indian merchant in Nepal. When his boss's business grew and expanded to Hong Kong, he got the rarest chance of joining him and never looked back. He worked tacitly under the tutelage of his Indian boss for years, learned and perfected the trade with hard work, and when he was finally ready, both mentally and legally, he started his own business. He had been running the grocery store since then. Most of his goods came from his old suppliers, the others he imported directly from India and Nepal, and he had been catering to the needs of the local diaspora society since then. With time, business had flourished, he owned the shop his family lived in and two more stores in other parts of Hong Kong. Life was good. His stores mostly sold goods brought in from South Asia since his customers were mostly South Asians, which was the main reason his shop didn't look similar to the other shops nearby. The father of the Sharma family was a good businessman. He knew how to make his customers happy and keep them coming back. When he started this first shop as a new business, he had always found it the lucky one. Since he never wanted to move away from there, he had been living in the same old place ever since.

Laxmi means wealth; it was an auspicious name. Laxmi Sharma was a tall, mild-mannered and fair-complexioned lady with an oval-shaped face, big eyes and a long nose. She had a long, black silky hair always braided in a single plait with a red ribbon.

Her attire had always been simple and traditional, whether it was a scorching hot summer day or a cold chilly winter one, she had never set foot outside without a shawl wrapped around her head and shoulders. She worked tirelessly at home; taking care of her home and family was her main job, and the idea of taking an outside job was almost unimaginable. It was against her tradition. The Sharma women worked within the four walls of the house, and took care of the family for life. So much so that she didn't even tend to the shop at any time. The men always took care of the business outside the home, and she was hardly seen outside without her man. The mother of the Sharma household was a devoted wife and a caring mother and was happy to live in the shadow of her man.

Bishnu and Hari Sharma were the couple's two sons. Bishnu, the eldest son, had no choice but to follow in his father's footsteps. He was experienced enough to look after one of their shops on the outskirts of Hong Kong. Hari, the youngest son, was still studying. He wanted to become a doctor in Beijing. The elder brother was quiet, obedient and tame; the younger brother was loud, rebellious and wild. Both looked different too. The first son was closer to the father, the second closer to his mother. The eldest son was already married, apparently the marriage was arranged, and he was living with his new family at one of the family shops in the New Territories of Hong Kong. Since the youngest son's studies were not complete, although he was in his final year, he was always away from home. The absence of the sons of the Sharma family created an unnecessary vacuum at home, especially during the festive seasons.

Ganga and Radha Sharma were the two precious daughters of the Sharma household. Ganga, the eldest, was married to a man chosen by her parents. Her husband was taking care of the second shop on the outskirts of Hong Kong. Radha, the youngest and dearest child of the family, had just started university and was still living with her parents at home as a princess.

Chapter 6

On the corner between Jaffe Road and Luard Road in Wan Chai, there was a small restaurant with an entrance made of a dark brown wooden carving. There were three rows of tables in a straight line. Each table, which had two armchairs, was covered with a white tablecloth with a scented candle and a menu in the middle. The cash register was situated near the main entrance, the kitchen was at the back, and there was a small stage at the back, next to the kitchen door. The restaurant had low lighting and was cosy. All the walls and glass windows were adorned with carvings, beautiful pictures of the majestic Himalayas, and metal ornaments probably from Nepal. Mild Nepali music played in the background continuously. It was a typical Nepalese restaurant widely found in Hong Kong. This one was small, but it had been serving authentic Nepalese and Indian food to the locals for years. It had a head cook, his assistant, a cleaner, a waiter, the owner and his wife – altogether six personnel. It opened daily for business at three in the afternoon, got busier mostly at dinnertime, and usually closed before midnight. Most of the customers came regularly since the food was good, simple and reasonably priced. The small restaurant was doing well.

Manohar means handsome; BK was his surname in short. Manohar BK was a polite, tall and handsome man, and like his name, he hailed from East Nepal and came to Hong Kong as an executive chef of a famous Indian restaurant chain. He learned his trade in New Delhi while staying with his maternal uncle there. He befriended an Indian from the diaspora who was visiting India from Hong Kong. Through Manohar's good cooking while he was visiting India, his new friend hired him as a chef for his new restaurant in Hong Kong. Manohar BK worked for his Indian boss for the next fifteen years in Hong Kong, and got himself established there with his family. When his boss finally let him go, he started his own small restaurant in Hong Kong. He had been working there ever since. Besides running his restaurant, he was an avid music lover, and always entertained his guests with good music

Parvati Biswakarma had a small but distinct face, curly hair and a swarthy complexion. Her petite body was deemed small even by Asian standards, and she was bestowed with a sharp tongue and a shrill voice. Due to her humble beginning, she loved money a bit too much and working behind the cash register at the restaurant was her favourite job. Their marriage was an arranged one, when she and her husband were quite young and both of their children were actually born in Nepal. She and the children joined him eventually in Hong Kong when he could afford a place. Their simple two-bedroom apartment was on the fourth floor of the same building as the restaurant, and they had been running the family restaurant quite adroitly since then.

Michael Biswakarma was the first-born. He had inherited his looks, hair and body structure from his mother's side, hence he was not as tall as his father. He also happened to be quite talkative for a man. Being the primogeniture of the family, the onus was on him to look after the restaurant in his father's absence, and he did help as an obligation, but social work was his favourite job. He liked meeting different people, talking about their daily social issues, and took pride in finding solutions for them. In contrast, Donna Biswakarma was tall and slender and had a nice face with a fair complexion framed by long black hair. She was far less talkative than her sibling but was a strong, confident and independent young woman. She had little interest in girly things and eventually wanted to be an activist journalist in the future.

Children of the BK family were modern. Unlike their parents, they harboured strong objections towards early marriage, and were opinionated. Hence the parents' wish of an early marriage for both had not been fulfilled yet and had been put on the backburner.

Chapter 7

The union of a Gurung, a Thapa, a Sharma and a Biswakarma was odd and remarkable at the same time. The union was quite an achievement and only possible in a foreign land like Hong Kong when simply having the same nationality means a lot for all.

'We have seen too much rain this year in Hong Kong!' Ram Bahadur said. He wasn't addressing anyone in particular.

'Rain makes our life miserable at the construction site,' Sher Bikram Thapa expressed his dislike with a gulp from a canned beer.

'The pork meat looks really fresh. I am cutting it into small and equal sizes, and the Bhutuwa (special fried fresh meat) will be really great today,' Krishna Sharma said, all the while drooling at the prospect of a nice treat. The thought of all that food prompted unprecedented salivation that had to be gulped down with a mouthful of cold beer. Since he was not good at cooking, the cutting and chopping of meat and vegetables were his main contribution, and he had perfected the newly acquired skill through practice.

'The taste between this and the bought one is completely different,' Manohar BK joined in with a beer can in hand. He was the unofficial cook. Cooking had not started yet. 'By the way, how did you get the fresh pork? I wasn't aware that our people get it directly from the farm.'

'It was a practice we started in the New Territories when we were still in the army,' Sher Bikram Thapa explained with pride. 'It was especially for Dashain, the meat-eating festival. We had a group of five to six people from the Shek Kong married quarters, and went to the nearby pig farms at Kam Tin, where we bought a pig or two, killed it, and shared the fresh meat among the families. We still have some old friends in Hong Kong and we get together sometimes to carry out the old tradition. It was from the same lot.'

'That is unbelievable!' Manohar BK couldn't hide his astonishment. 'I thought that every meat we get in Hong Kong was from the slaughter house. Where do you get to perform such jobs? You don't get in trouble with the police?'

'Of course, it is all possible in the New Territories.' Sher Bikram Thapa divulged all the details since he was desperate to talk about it. 'It is normally done in the bush, near the farm. Once the animal is killed, we make a small fire to burn the skin, and then cut it into small pieces using a khukri. The freshly cut meat is then packed into plastic bags and carried in a zebra bag. It is that simple.'

'And you never had any problem at all with that?' Even Krishna Sharma was curious and pitched in. Manohar BK had served him as well as the other two with a new can of beer and they started drinking again.

'Normally, it was done during night-time, so, it is not a problem at all,' Sher Bikram Thapa said with an impish look. 'But we got caught by the Hong Kong police once. They got suspicious when blood was dripping out of the zebra bag, but let us go once we explained the matter to them in great detail. It was in fact quite scary and we all got nervous. The police told us it was illegal to kill animals on our own and not to do it again. We are more cautious now and we only do it once or twice a year.'

'If it is illegal, we shouldn't do it again then,' Ram Bahadur said.

'Is it true that some Nepalese people killed some wild buffalos in Kam Tin? I am not sure, but I heard it somewhere on the news and I thought that was quite absurd,' Manohar BK inquired with the curious eyes of a child.

'Yes, I also heard it somewhere and I think it was on Dashain,' (Nepal's main festival) Krishna Sharma added to what Manohar BK had already started.

'I think it was true and that was not the right thing to do,' It was the idealistic Ram Bahadur talking. 'As we are in Hong Kong, we must act like Hongkongers.'

'They must be thinking they were still in Nepal, ha…!' Manohar BK commented.

'Typical Nepalese mentality!' Krishna Sharma lamented without explaining what he actually meant and got himself busy with the task at hand.

'How do you want me to cut the Choi Sum?' Ram Bahadur asked. He was the only one in the group who didn't drink and one can of soda was already enough.

'Let me do all the cutting, bro. It is my job. Please don't bother,' Krishna Sharma remonstrated. He was almost done with the meat cutting.

'Maybe I can help on preparing onion, garlic and ginger then,' Ram Bahadur suggested. He wanted to pitch in.

'Don't worry, bro. It is all covered. We have plenty of time and I will do it all.' Krishna Sharma was adamant and he didn't let others interrupt his cooking.

'I will fix the rice cooker then,' Ram Bahadur said as he got up, fetched the rice cooker and started cleaning it before filling it up with enough rice and water. He showed it to Manohar BK to make sure that it was the proper quantity, plugged it into the electric socket on the wall and turned the switch on.

'Is there anything that I can do to help?' Sher Bikram Thapa asked. His tone was tinged with guilt as he knew everyone was working except him.

'Relax, everything is covered,' Krishna Sharma assured him.

'Please cut two pieces of fresh onion and some tomatoes as well. One for the Bhutuwa and another for the tomato chutney, thanks!' Manohar BK reminded Krishna Sharma and started peeling garlic at the same time.

'Once the preparation is done, only the cooking remains, and we all know who does all the cooking here,' Krishna Sharma replied with a carefree smile and went back to the cutting job as he had been doing until now.

It was almost five in the afternoon and outside it was cloudy and calm but there was no rain. Once the chopping was over, Manohar BK started the preparation for the cooking and the others remained seated on the floor. After some time, when the cooking was almost done, the entire place was replete with a nice aroma of freshly cooked food. Manohar BK was indeed a talented cook and nobody was disappointed.

The meal was finally served on a platter, which held nicely cooked aromatic rice, fresh pork meat with Choi Sum, and onion tomato chutney served hot and fresh straight from the oven. They all sat on the floor in the lotus position, got enough servings of cold beer on the side and started eating with their hands – the most traditional yet gratifying way of enjoying good food. No wonder there was no exchange of words until their plates were completely emptied and all cravings for magnificent food were satisfied.

Krishna Sharma was the one who always enjoyed eating from the cooking wok, and only the charred taste of the wok could satisfy his craving. The extra work he did to guarantee that reward was cutting vegetables beforehand and washing the big wok afterwards. In comparison to the gratifying end, it was nothing.

After the heavy meal, some would lean against the wall, the others would lie down and the real conversation would finally start and would not end until 11 p.m. It was the time they had to stop if they were to catch the last train for home. Especially Sher Bikram Thapa, who lived on Yuen Long. He had to rush for the last train. The other three had no such hassle as they lived nearby, but they preferred coming and going at the same time.

'The Bhutuwa is by far the best I have had recently.' Krishna Sharma declared.

'I couldn't agree more!' Sher Bikram Thapa said as he felt his bulging stomach.

'He must be one of the best male cooks I have ever met. Hands down!' Ram Bahadur said with pride and leaned back against the wall.

'That's why he owns one of the best restaurants in Hong Kong!' Krishna Sharma raised a toast and the other two followed suit.

'Enough praising, you guys are making me blush again!' Manohar BK said, actually blushing. They were really having a good time.

'Everybody is leaving for the UK. What is this all about? Do you guys have any plans of moving there as well?' Krishna Sharma asked as he initiated a new topic. He was the most inquisitive among the group and the new bug must have caught him as well.

'It seemed like a new trend nowadays in Hong Kong,' Manohar BK said. 'Many from my circle of people have already left and more are leaving soon.'

'I haven't thought about it yet,' Sher Bikram Thapa replied. 'It took almost a decade or so for us to settle down here, and I am not sure how to start from scratch there. I don't know if finding a job is harder or not there.' He seemed uncertain.

'Me too, I think life is much better here in Hong Kong.' Ram Bahadur seemed unexcited about the prospect of moving to the UK. 'Finding suitable jobs for us are not hard here, plenty of security and construction work is easily available, and that should be enough for a simple life like ours.'

'Not to mention the weather. They said the English weather is terrible,' Manohar BK said with clinched teeth as if he were actually feeling the chill.

'That is actually true. When we were posted in the UK, we used to insert three sets of plastic bags between the sock and the boot, and we could still not feel our feet.' Sher Bikram Thapa remembered his old army days as if it were yesterday.

'Unlike here, they just have two seasons there in the UK, summer and winter. The winter is cold, wet and dark. It never stops raining. The days are shorter and people hardly venture outside. But the summer is warm; the days are longer and beautiful. Most noticeably, the whole place blossoms as if it were, in fact, the Garden of Eden and people are almost everywhere. I think our people, especially the seniors, might suffer in the winter.' Ram Bahadur Gurung was happy that he could share his own experience of the great English weather with his friends and he could not have said it better.

'They said people don't have to work hard as we do here, the government provides all sorts of allowances there, and you can live on it without even working,' Krishna Sharma said with a twinkle in his eyes and it clearly effused unintended envy.

'They have, but I am not sure exactly how much. Although it is pretty common in developed nations, living on government handouts is definitely not the way of life that I want to have. Even so, I don't know whether it will be enough or not,' said the idealist Ram Bahadur Gurung in a philosophical manner.

'After serving the Goras for more than two centuries, we fully deserved that and the British should take care of all the former Gurkha soldiers and their families for the rest of their lives.' Manohar BK got emotional while he was saying it. Everybody in the community was well aware of how the British have treated the Gurkhas unfairly for so long a time. Gurkhas vented their anger but always when they knew they wouldn't be heard and therefore there would be no repercussions.

'Who asked us to be so poor and weak?' Sher Bikram Thapa asked with a big sigh.

'There is no bigger curse than to be a poor man in this world,' Ram Bahadur Gurung agreed. 'Thieves and crooks live a more dignified life than a poor man, and nice men always come in last. It seems that the whole world runs on money alone.'

'It seems that all of the former Gurkhas and their families will eventually move to the UK soon,' Krishna Sharma conjectured but it ended up sounding like a statement.

'They are going to the UK to test the waters and if it doesn't work out well, they might come back to Hong Kong again. We want to keep both options open, you know,' Manohar BK said with an impish look and he wasn't wrong.

'They are not selling everything off here, at least for now,' Sher Bikram Thapa said.

'That is a smart choice.' Ram Bahadur Gurung couldn't agree more.

It was already dark outside and thousands of neon lights brightened up Hong Kong's streets and buildings. The men had changed positions many times and were rolling around on the floor as if they were fully fed and satiated babies.

'I don't think I can make it next week and thought that I would let you all know,' Manohar BK said with a rather serious demeanour and waited for others to talk.

'What is it? Hope all is fine,' Ram Bahadur Gurung asked with concern.

'Nothing serious, it is just the usual community meeting again.' He sounded peeved.

'One day it is a community meeting, and then a village meeting, a region meeting, Numbari meeting, a regiment meeting, a family meeting… the list can go on and on,' Krishna Sharma exclaimed. 'We have so many organizations here that if we attend all of them, we will never have a free weekend in a whole year and it won't even be enough then.'

'Why do we Nepalese people have so many organizations in Hong Kong? We are only good at making new organizations,' Sher Bikram Thapa said with a shaking head.

'Because we like talking!' Manohar BK chipped in.

'Only talking but no action!' Krishna Sharma butted in.

'Regardless of audiences or no audiences, we just want a platform,' Ram Bahadur Gurung added. 'If we cannot talk here, create another one.'

'Talking garbage with no responsibility!' Sher Bikram Thapa nailed it.

'Talk is cheap but action needs courage,' Manohar BK said.

'Our society is so badly divided that nothing can work out as a team,' Krishna Sharma said, sighing. 'We might have a separate organization for each hundred people, and that is the reason why we can never become a stronger force.'

'We are already a minority here and I don't think we can ever be the one united group here in Hong Kong.' Manohar BK couldn't agree more.

'Our outdated feudal caste system is the main root of our divided society. A Gurung can never support a Rai, a Limbu, a Tamang or a Magar. So much so that there are two types of Gurung within itself and the village and region, and relationships also play a big part in dividing those within the Gurung community. What else is there to say?' Ram Bahadur Gurung concluded in his explanation of why there wouldn't be a single and united community within the Nepalese people.

'It is in our blood and wherever we go, it follows us,' Sher Bikram Thapa summarized the pathetic but true situation of the Nepalese people.

'No wonder our country is always languishing,' Krishna Sharma said, concluding the conversation.

'I am really happy that it is not affecting our friendship and despite coming from different castes and backgrounds, we are still together.' Manohar BK wanted to lighten up the atmosphere that had rather become sombre and sad by now.

Everyone agreed with a slight nod and silence prevailed for some time.

'We live in Hong Kong, which is such a nice and advanced place. If you have the desire and determination, anything is possible here. But look at our situation here, we are still stuck in the back alley of our life in Nepal, and nobody tries to come out of it willingly. We all came here seeking a better life, opportunities are right in front of us, and yet, we don't even know how to grab them. Someone has rightly said: 'We are always running after the wrong target. We live in Hong Kong but never stop living the same old life that we so desperately wanted to improve. That is the irony as well as truth of our life,' Ram Bahadur Gurung said scathingly. It was clear that all these feelings had been smothering inside of him for quite some time and he was quite relieved when it was finally done.

'Yes, no matter where we go, we don't stop talking about dirty politics back in Nepal, and that is another specialty of the Nepalese people,' Krishna Sharma concluded.

'We are not only irretrievably divided but also experts at leg-pulling,' Manohar BK said sarcastically.

'If it is not for me, nobody else can have it either, ha, ha, ha…!' Sher Bikram Thapa laughed out loud. He was laughing to himself.

'And most of all, that "what is in it for me" sort of attitude before anything else,' Krishna Sharma added his bit with a sad and defeated smile.

'That we are here in a foreign land says it all. Nothing happens without reason and no one but us are the ones at fault for our current situation,' Ram Bahadur Gurung said with a force that made it seem as if he was delivering a speech to a crowd.

'Our people want power without responsibility,' Krishna Sharma continued.

'What do we call the country run by thieves?' Manohar BK pondered as he tried to find the right word to explain what he was trying to say.

'Kleptocracy!' Krishna Sharma helped out.

'That is a better way to describe it. We cannot after all say thieves openly, right?' Manohar BK asked as he needed approval from all and everybody duly nodded.

'Sadly, that is our homeland,' Sher Bikram Thapa said with a sigh.

'No wonder it is also called the cursed nation,' Ram Bahadur Gurung agreed.

A protracted silence lingered on for quite a while. The night had matured by now and it was time to return home. They reluctantly got up, cleaned the dishes and tidied up the place as well. When they finally locked up the place and went down the staircase, it was almost 11 p.m. They stopped at the main entrance again, bid each other goodbye and went their respective ways. The night market at Temple Street was as busy and crowded as it had always been and, before too long, they had all disappeared into the crowd.

Chapter 8

He woke up precisely at 4 p.m., took a shower and wore the uniform that he had been wearing for the last few years on a daily basis. As a night security guard, Ram Bahadur Gurung would return home before 7.30 a.m., take some light food, and go to sleep. Sleeping in broad daylight was not easy initially even when the door and windows were closed and the curtains fully drawn. But he got accustomed to the odd habit subsequently, and had had no problems ever since. He was served early dinner at 5 p.m. and he would leave the house precisely at 5.30 p.m. The shopping mall where he had been working for the last five years was located within a fifteen-minute walk, and he would always arrive at work fifteen minutes before actual duty hour – 6 p.m. Being punctual was one of the disciplines he had learned from army training, and it was something that would remain with him for the rest of his life, and it was appreciated too.

When he had early dinner the husband and the wife would have the chance to discuss matters with other family members and find solutions if necessary.

'No need to make so many dishes every day,' he said to his dutiful wife as he sat down and glanced around the dinner table. Affection was hidden under his chiding. She perfectly understood and didn't say a word as she got busy in the kitchen.

Dinner was steamed fish, a bowl full of white rice, a green vegetable and lentils. He picked up the rice bowl with his left hand and grabbed the chopstick by his right hand to start with the fish. Unlike other Nepalese people, he always preferred using a chopstick instead of his hand.

'Do you know what this fish is called?' He started the conversation as usual.

'I am not sure but it might be a red carp,' Gauri Maya Gurung replied.

'Did it look red prior to being cooked?' He asked, childlike enthusiasm evident on his face.

'It was a mixture of yellow and red,' she explained.

'They all taste the same to me. I think it is the other ingredients that you mix with it that create the final taste, and whatever you make will always taste great.' He had learned the art of flattery very late in life, but each word he said was as true as the morning dew.

'We Nepalese cannot differentiate a good fish from a bad one,' she said in a firm voice, as flattery had no effect at all on her. 'But that is not our fault. Since we have no ocean near us, we don't know much about seafood.'

'You are absolutely right,' he agreed. 'Most of us are also scared of fish bones, hence we eat less fish.' He spoke with food in his mouth.

'Our way of life is mostly determined by our location,' she said from the kitchen.

'Hope you have kept enough for yourself and Anmol,' he said.

'Don't worry. You please have food to your fill otherwise you will feel hungry during the night.' She wanted to make sure that he went to work with a full stomach. He knew she cared for him and they both fully understood it. 'If we don't eat and rest properly, what is the point of working so hard? And staying awake the whole night is not an easy task after all,' she said it in a soft voice as she was talking to no one but herself. He didn't say a word and kept on eating.

'By the way, when is your rest day for this week?' she asked as she remembered something important and needed his help.

'As usual, it is next Wednesday, why?' He was surprised and looked at her.

'Is it possible to make it on Saturday instead?' she asked.

'I can talk with the supervisor and see if it can be arranged. What is it?' He got interested and looked at her intently.

'Oh, the usual get-together thing. It is the birthday party of my nephew's son and we are all invited. If we can all go together, it would be nice,' she said it with a disinterested expression on her face, but he knew it was important. Since he was not a fan of such gatherings, it was mostly her who fulfilled the family's social obligations, and he knew he had to lend some help occasionally.

'I will check and tell you as soon as I can,' he replied in a rather convincing voice that not only surprised her but also him as well, and they smiled.

'Sometimes it is a birthday, the other time it is weaning day, an anniversary, a wedding, a gathering in a village or region, and so on,' she said as a matter of fact and continued with a sigh. 'I have already turned down many, attended some on my own, and had to make few more excuses to keep the other side happy. But this one is unavoidable. If we don't attend it, they might get offended and I really do hope that you can make it.'

'I will do my best. I think it should be okay. In the worst case, I will ask my colleagues and see if we can exchange the holiday among ourselves. Don't worry,' he said with an assurance that inevitably made both happy and relieved.

He had almost finished dinner by now, and she was readying his backpack while they talked. It had a thermos filled with vegetable juice in summer and hot milk tea in winter, a plastic water bottle, an apple and a pack of digestive biscuits.

'How was the day for Anmol today?' He sounded like he had just remembered to ask but in reality, it was the routine that he had never failed to perform. They had decided not only to talk less about him during any conversation but also treat it as one of the trivial issues of the family. By making the perennial issue less significant, it became much more attainable and prevented insanity.

'We did some reading, drawing, TV watching as well as house cleaning. He is perfectly fine and calm today. He is resting in his room now,' she explained, finding solace in this daily routine. Without it their days wouldn't pass. They had been doing it for the last twenty years and more, but she said it with the same oomph and enthusiasm as if it was the very first time and it didn't sound jaded at all.

'Did you hear anything from Trimol lately?' He asked only as a matter of routine. He was the least one to worry about for them and they both knew it.

'He hasn't called for some time now. I think they are simply too busy and there is nothing to be worried about.' She had a readymade answer that she had already used a few more times before. The other son was not only smart, strong and independent but also down to earth. He also had a new wife and a new life, and when your new wife doesn't belong to the same race and community, it was hard to fit in.

He finished dinner without saying anything, cleared up the remainder and walked to the bathroom. After the quick clean up, he picked up the backpack, checked on Anmol through the slightly open door, said goodbye to his wife, and headed out. She followed him to the door and watched him until he walked out of her sight. As she closed the door and returned to the kitchen, it was precisely 5.30 p.m.

Chapter 9

It was one of those rare mornings when both were still at home. Sher Bikram Thapa had a change in schedule and he was reporting late for work. Gita Thapa had a day off and she was planning to visit one of her friends in the afternoon. It was a nice morning with a clear sky. As there was still sometime before the monsoon rain, the days were long and bright and the temperature was rising. Since both girls were already married and living away with their respective new families, Sher and Gita were the only two still living there and the place was as quiet and humdrum as an elderly home.

'You should have rested longer,' she said as she gave him a mug of hot chocolate.

'Old habits don't die,' he said as he cautiously sipped hot chocolate from the mug and sat on the chair in the living room.

'It must have been quite a while since we had breakfast together, right?' she said with a nostalgic look and started arranging the food on the table. There was toasted bread, butter, fried eggs, long fried sausage and borsch soup.

It was a typical breakfast that they had discovered since their days in the army camp. Just like most of the ex-servicemen and their families, they also liked this type of foreign breakfast and tried it whenever they had the time to prepare it.

'Please start when it is still hot and fresh,' she said and sat opposite him.

'Not even half of all the soldiers would have breakfast at the army camp,' he said as he picked up a slice of hot bread and added butter on it. He continued, 'But I would never miss them. It was my favourite and despite having it on a daily basis for so long, I never got tired of it, and I still like it as much as I used to then.'

'I tried to find the baked beans but supermarkets here don't have them,' she lamented and started sipping the borsch soup with a spoon.

'It was only flat bread that we could take as much as we wanted. The others were served by the cookhouse staffs and we hardly asked twice,' he said with the borrowed words from his memory. He felt like it was just yesterday.

'It has already been so many years,' she agreed and said emotionally, 'Time flies but memories remain forever.'

'Yes, it was just like yesterday. Do you remember? We used to eat the same thing when we were at the married quarters,' he said, his face bright like a child.

'We bought what we knew the best, I suppose,' she said, and they laughed together at their own naivety and simple way of life.

'Do you remember aloo dam? (A typical dish with potato and spices). It must be the most popular dish of the army camp and it was served on each and every occasion of any party or gathering throughout our time in the army.' He was still in a joyful mood and those past memories from his army life provided more than enough fuel to prolong it for a bit longer.

'Who doesn't know aloo dam? There was no party without it and everyone knew it by heart, including the wives,' she replied with a smile.

'You know what? We even had someone nicknamed aloo dam

in our battalion and we used to enjoy a great laugh at his expense.' He couldn't hide his excitement and expressed it by chortling in a childlike manner.

'Was he aware of his nickname? He must have been so mad!' she said as if she had heard it for the very first time. Needless to say, it was not the first time.

'Of course, he knew, and he was also a member of our laughing club,' he said casually. 'Army life provides camaraderie that civilian life lacks. Nobody minds such things.' He actually had wanted to say that joking around and laughing at each other was one of the ways of coping with the tough and physical life in the army – but he hadn't been able to do it.

'Our communities still serve aloo dam, even at gatherings nowadays,' she said. 'The practice must have come from the army days for sure.'

'Aloo dam with anchovy is still my favourite,' he couldn't resist adding.

'I will certainly make that for you the next time.' She knew his intention. 'By the way, now I remember, I will be going to my friend's place this afternoon. They are having a silver jubilee party and we are invited.'

'Where do they live? Hope it is not that far away. You know I cannot come as I will still be at work then,' he explained while putting the whole egg in his mouth.

'It would have been nice if we could go together, but work is work and I will explain that to them. Don't worry,' she said in a reserved voice and drank more soup.

'As we were saying...' He stopped as he remembered something and continued. 'Nepalese communities in Hong Kong have so many organizations and groups that if we were to attend all the functions they hosted, we would have no time for other things. It is the Magar (one of the main castes) community, the village community and then the district and zonal communities, followed by intake, company and regimental community from the army side, which add more communities related to our job, hobbies and society. Our people are experts at creating communities. No wonder the country is so divided and has no unity.'

'I know, but we cannot avoid them all. There are few such gatherings, which we must attend, and the one tonight is one of them,' she explained.

'One Nepalese writer who knew China very well said this. Our people from Eastern Nepal are like the Northerners in China and the Southerners in China are like our people from Western Nepal. The people from North China talk about country, patriotism and politics. On the contrary, the people from South China talk about money, self-development and business. But I would say our people only talk about dirty politics.' Sher said this and it was clear that he did not sound like his own self.

It was not only Gita but Sher who surprised himself. He could hardly believe what he had just heard. They both needed some time before being able to act normal.

'That is so true,' she finally managed to say and wondered where he had learned to talk like that. The simple and humdrum army guy suddenly started talking like an expert and that certainly took her by surprise.

'Did you buy some gift?' he asked. The sudden aberration on his part totally caught her off guard and she ended up blabbering before she could calm down and respond.

'Gift…oh yes, gift. I have bought earrings for her and a jacket for him,' she eventually said.

'You women know better than us in such matters. I am sure

that you have thought it through.' He shrugged off the potential responsibility easily. Men are good at that, she thought and she wasn't wrong at all.

'Yes, I have,' she managed to reply. 'Besides, it's like an exchange of gifts among a group of children. Everybody takes turns. If I bring earrings and a jacket for them this time, they will return similar or better gifts when it's our turn, and the chain continues until everyone within the group gets their turn. So, there is nothing to worry about.'

'Pity that some cheapskates won't always follow the rules,' he warned.

'Then, in that case, nobody will attend their event again,' she commented.

'Yes, it is still unavoidable,' he said and she also agreed. For the next few minutes, they ate in utter silence and that particular discussion was over once and for all.

'Do you want more?' she asked as he emptied the mug. He shook his head to indicate a 'no', and she ought to have known better. Regardless of the weather conditions, the only drink he had been taking for the last fifteen years was nothing but hot chocolate milk. It had been a daily ritual that he couldn't go without. He started drinking it as a strength drink as his job required at the beginning, and it had never changed since then.

'Did you hear anything from the girls lately?' he asked as he helped to clear the table and taking the used plates back to the kitchen.

'I spoke to them last night on the phone,' she replied and started tidying up the kitchen. 'Just leave them there on the sink. No need to wash them. I have enough time to clear that out. Don't worry,' she said, pointing at the used dishes.'

'I will wash them, don't worry. I have enough time,' he

insisted and carried on with the washing job by ignoring her. Once the girls had left home, they had only each other for company and whenever he had the time, he would pitch in and help her with household chores. Washing dishes and cleaning clothes were the two main things he did to help her, and as an ex-Gurkha soldier, he never shirked his responsibilities but always gave 200 per cent to his duty. Furthermore, he always felt sorry for his beloved wife. She happened to be not only playing for the zonal basketball team but also captaining the team. Had she not been married to him and followed him, her chance of representing the national team was just a matter of time. She was quite famous as well as respected and had a substantial number of followers of her own. Sadly for now, she was the team leader of six old women whose job was to clean and tidy up the roadsides back in rural Kam Tin village and it was all because of him. The guilt plagued him persistently and helping her with household chores was the least he could do for her. He knew it was nothing in comparison to her sacrifices but it did certainly make him feel that he was at least trying.

'Rekha said they were planning to open her own beauty parlour.' Unaware of what he was thinking, she continued, 'She said she will invite us when it is all fixed, money is not a problem, and they still have to decide between a few more places. She said it might be somewhere in the East Tsim Sha Tsui.'

'That white guy seems to have all the solutions to her problem,' he said in a passive tone.

'Don't speak like that, he is our son-in-law, after all,' she remonstrated.

'Goras are a blessed breed, it is their rule and they survive wherever they go.' It was actually a compliment but. Sher made it seem like he pitied them.

'Nobody can do anything to change their fate, what is written is bound to happen,' she said in a resigned voice.

'All I can say is I hope she is happy,' he said out of love for his daughter. She couldn't agree more and nodded in complete agreement.

A few more minutes passed in silence and the only sounds that could be heard were the clanking of plates and the running of water.

'Disha said she was working at the hotel now as an assistant to the chef,' Gita said in a less enthusiastic voice than before. 'Money is okay but she can learn a lot, and it is an excellent opportunity for her future. Not sure what he was doing but she said he was fine and everything is going well.'

'Never sure of what those black men are doing,' he continued in an indifferent tone.

'It is the fate not the face that must be bright in life,' she said, trying to defend the indefensible one, but her shaky voice gave away her own doubts and insecurity.

'I am sorry but that is not happening,' he was convinced.

'Nobody can predict the future by looking at a face,' she said, while trying to appear strong.

'We will wait and see,' he said with full confidence. He had already finished cleaning up the dishes by now and he was drying his hands with a clean towel. 'Look, I am not biased. I always speak my mind and nothing is hidden from both of us. Of course, I mean well for both my daughters. What kind of fathers don't? But there is a huge difference between actually wanting something and the reality, and we both know what the reality is. I hope time can prove us wrong and change her fate for good.'

They both knew there was no point of any more discussion. They remained quiet and got busy doing whatever they were doing at that moment.

'What time are you leaving for work?' Gita, said, finally breaking the silence.

'I will leave around 10.30 a.m.,' he replied and went to switch on the TV.

'I will pack your lunch box before then,' she said and kept on working.

'Don't worry about my dinner,' he said without looking at her. 'I assume you will be having dinner at your friend's place and I will fix something light for myself when I am back. Besides, I will be late anyway. You have a good time, okay?'

'I hope so. I will return as soon as I can. It will probably be late though,' she said and carried on working on her own. He sat on the sofa and watched TV. The day had matured and the hot wind outside had started piercing through the window.

Chapter 10

It was almost three in the afternoon, the weather was hot and humid, and the shop had hardly any customers. Despite the hot weather, only the shop area was air-conditioned and there were fans in the remaining portions of the house. Krishna Sharma, the shop owner, was firmly seated behind the counter, and as always, nothing inside the shop went unnoticed by his eagle eye. Since the youngest daughter was away at university, only Laxmi Sharma, the matriarch, was at home doing the household chores as usual.

'Here is your afternoon tea,' Laxmi said as she placed a big round cup, which had a cap and a handle, in front of him and politely asked, 'Would you like to have some biscuits with the tea or something else?'

He grabbed the cup, opened it and sipped some hot tea with a slurping sound. It was a special homemade ginger tea mixed with clove, cinnamon, thick milk and sugar. He needed it at least three times a day – once early in the morning, at three in the afternoon and right before bedtime. His days started and ended with it. People are said to have difficulty sleeping if they have tea right before bedtime. But it was the opposite for him.

'Just bring something,' he said without even looking at her and took a few more sips. A customer came in and started checking out things around the shop. Laxmi waited for a few more moments and eventually went inside the shop.

The phone rang and Krishna answered it. It was his first son, Bishnu Sharma, at the other end. 'Namaste, namaste,' Krishna said and asked, 'So what time will you be at the airport then?'

'Around 5.50 p.m. I should be returning home before 6.30 p.m.,' his son replied.

'That is only if the plane arrives on time,' Krishna said sarcastically. 'We know how they work in Nepal.'

'They said it is on time, Father. I sincerely do hope it is.' The son sounded hopeful.

'They always say that,' Krishna smirked. 'Anyway… make sure you have checked all your stuff before leaving the airport. You got the list, right?'

'Yes, Father. Please don't worry,' the son assured him. 'I was planning to come to Jordan first, then to sister's shop followed by my place at the end. What do you say, Father?'

'No, no, you will have to make a big unnecessary roundabout,' he harrumphed. He wasn't worrying about the well-being of his offspring but the petrol wastage. 'Ask the airline guy to deliver our stuff here on his way back, and you just go to sister's place first and then to your place. Don't waste your time. Do as I tell you, okay.'

'Okay, Father, I will talk to him. I hope he won't refuse.' The son wasn't so sure.

'Of course, he won't,' Krishna assured him. 'If you have any problem, just call me. After what we did for him, he won't dare to refuse for sure. Have some faith.'

'I will, Father. Please don't worry. Now I have to go,' the son replied.

'Okay, keep updating me,' his father reminded him.

'Namaste, Father, bye!' the son said before he hung up.

'Bye!' Krishna said as he ended the conversation with a satisfying look and continued to drink his favourite tea.

While they were still talking, Laxmi had already brought in a plate of biscuits and left it on the counter. It was a digestive biscuit from Nepal.

Since most of his regular customers were from Nepal and people from other South Asian nations, all the goods he had in the shop were to their liking and had to be brought in from Nepal. Not by choice but out of necessity, they had to forge a nice, strong connection with the airline people. Flying in goods from Nepal by paying the regular price was not a viable option and an alternative scheme had been devised.

We all know that planes were not always full, especially flying from Kathmandu to Hong Kong. Passengers hardly have any luggage and the plane flew almost empty. As planned, traders started filling up the empty spaces with new goods from Nepal and sold them through newly popped-up grocery shops in Hong Kong. As a result, everything was as easily available in Hong Kong as in Kathmandu, and planes also didn't have to fly empty anymore. It was a win-win situation for all those who were involved, except the airline itself. The catch was something more sinister. All the income the airline had earned through the newly fangled businesses were allegedly going, not to the airline itself, but into the pockets of its scheming staff. In order to keep the straying traders quiet, they were sold much cheaper than the market price. When both conniving sides were benefitting, the chance of betrayal was very rare and their conscience was blurred. Nepalese, especially those in the higher and powerful posts, are very good at it.

A few more customers visited the shop, bought their desired goods and left.

As he wanted to savour the special ginger tea, he was taking time to finish it and that was the reason why it was always served in a vacuumed cup with an airtight cap. The cup was one of his favourite possessions, and he had always kept it in sight.

The mobile, which he had placed under the counter, suddenly vibrated. He put the mobile on vibration because he didn't like the sound of the phone ringing and wished that he could have put the landline phone on vibration as well. Glancing at the mobile brightened his face and prompted him to answer it. It was Hari Sharma, the other son who was studying in Beijing.

'Why don't you call my home number?' Krishna chided even before the formality of asking about his son's well-being. It was his unique way of expressing affection, a shibboleth that only the family members understood, and didn't mind. He also had a habit of speaking in half sentences and leaving the other half for the others to guess. What he actually intended to say was that calling the landline would have cost nothing, and that his son was wasting money by calling his father's mobile. What's more, Krishna was well known for his thrift; frugality ran in his blood.

'I am not talking long, Father. I just called to say hello and everything is fine,' his son replied. He completely understood that his father was a miser.

'Don't worry for us. Just make sure that you study well.' He sounded like most fathers out there who pretended they were as tough as nails. Emotions were for women, they never failed to remind themselves and continued to act tough.

'Is Mother around? Can I talk with her for a second? Hope my brother and sisters are all fine,' he asked as he wanted to make sure that he missed no one, and he was leaving no chances for other family members to voice their grievances.

'All is fine. Don't worry. I will tell them you had asked for them.' What he actually meant was: don't be a sissy and don't waste my money on such nonsense.

'Is Mom around? I just want to say hello,' the son repeated. He genuinely cared about her.

'She is fine. Don't worry. Spend wisely. Study hard and take very good care of yourself, okay. Now hang up!' He had no intention of prolonging the conversation.

'Okay, Namaste, Father, and take care,' the son said, reluctantly getting ready to hang up.

'Okay, be good!' Krishna said and ended the conversation. As he put down the phone and looked up, to his utter astonishment, he saw his wife standing in front of him. She had had a premonition that her son had called and had come running from the inside of the house so she could speak with him. Her excitement was crushed even before she could reach the phone.

He couldn't stand the look in her eyes and deliberately looked away. He needed some time before he could talk again and pretended that he was looking for something around the counter. Nothing was hidden from her experienced eyes and she knew exactly what was happening. But it was too late for a discussion. She took a long breath and simply said, 'Hope he is eating well, sleeping well and has enough money. Please let me talk with him when he calls again, and I won't take long.' Then she turned to walk back to disappear again behind the curtains.

He certainly felt bad and sorry for her and promised himself not to do that next time. However, by the time the son called again, he had already forgotten about the promises he had made to himself and ended up repeating the same mistake. This time though, he was determined to make it right and let them finally talk.

A few more customers came and went. The special ginger tea that he had been enjoying for the last hour and a half was finally finished, and he ended up flipping the TV channels searching for an interesting programme to watch. As he couldn't settle on one, he ended up watching a local news channel.

Then two Nepalese women entered the shop, both in typical Nepali attire – flowery sarongs, short-sleeved tops and a shawl – and carrying a brown shopping bag. They went through all the goods within the shop, picked their choices with much caution, and eventually walked to the counter. They were regulars and knew the owner well.

'Sahuji (shop owner in Nepali), here is my list. Please check,' the first woman said as she placed them on the counter. She had rice, lentils, onion, instant noodles, garlic, chilli powder, snacks, chickpea, biscuits, ghee and five pockets of spice.

'Total three-hundred thirty-five, please,' he said once he had checked carefully and fully calculated. The first lady started putting her purchases into the shopping bag.

'Now it is my turn, here is the list, Sahuji, and please check them,' the next lady requested while emptying them on top of the counter. She had rice, pulse, chickpeas, instant noodles, garlic, and onion, a few pockets of spice, snacks, five DVDs, two magazines and three types of Nepalese newspaper.

'Total three-hundred and eighty-five, please.' He declared the total value twice after checking the purchases carefully and waited until the second lady managed to pack them into the shopping bag she had carried with her. Since they were regular customers, he even helped pack her purchases and made sure they were properly placed inside the bag.

Once the bags were packed and placed to the side, he waited patiently for the ladies to make the final payment. But they seemed like they were not prepared and were looking around the shop. He waited, his eyes following their steps. After some time, the ladies picked up their respective bags and looked at him as if they were looking for permission to leave.

'It seems like the payment is not done, ha…!' he awkwardly said.

'No, we always buy with credit here' the first woman replied with a blush.

'Don't pretend you don't know about it, ha, ha, ha…' the second lady laughed.

'We thought that you have already put it on the books,' the first lady jumped in.

'I know, but please at least give me something,' he requested.

'It is not even the end of the month, Baba has no pay yet,' the second lady explained.

'This isn't the first time. Do you think we will run away?' the first lady added.

'It is a pittance for you,' the second lady reasoned.

'Don't worry! We will clear it all once we get the salary,' the first lady assured him.

'We are Nepali, remember!' Both ladies said together as they walked away before he could say anything in his defence. He couldn't believe what had just happened and started shaking his head in sheer annoyance.

'We live in one of the most advanced, sophisticated and civilized societies like Hong Kong, and yet, we cannot come out of our small world and never stop acting like we are still back in Nepal.' This was precisely what he intended to say, but forced by habit, he ended up saying, 'Our people never change!'

In the course of the next few hours, some more customers came and went intermittently and then it was almost 6 p.m. The first son was supposed to give him a call by now, he said to himself and decided to wait for a while before checking on him again. It was still hot and humid outside. The young daughter should have arrived home by now, he thought. The phone rang just then – it was the first son calling to inform him that all the arrangements had been made as planned. The wife was already busy preparing dinner as usual. The airline guy should be there by 8 p.m. He sat behind the counter with a sense of relief and tended to the shop as he had been doing for years. A few more customers had come in, bought something, and left. He hoped his younger daughter would return home soon and his day would have gone well by then.

Chapter 11

It was a lazy Sunday afternoon, the weather was still hot and humid, and outside it was as crowded and busy as it had always been. Unlike other Sunday afternoons, Manohar BK and Parvati BK were at home and that created an awkward situation for both. Had it not been for the pest control job, which was a mandatory requirement from the health and hygiene department that had ordered the closing, both would have already been at the restaurant by now and busied themselves in preparation of the timely opening at five. It must have been months, if not years, since they had spent a Sunday afternoon at home, and the new experience was already making them uncomfortable.

'Take it as a much-needed rest. I will make some herbal tea for both of us,' Parvati BK, who couldn't stand her husband's restlessness anymore, eventually spoke out.

'I am not accustomed to resting at home on a Sunday afternoon,' said Manohar BK, who couldn't hide his situation and frustration. 'It must have been a very long time, right?' he wondered aloud, but didn't stop pacing around the room.

'Please have this. They said natural herbs have a calming effect,' she said as she served him a freshly minted herbal tea in a nice-looking teacup with a saucer. After all, they were restaurateurs and had some knowledge about the business they were in.

He accepted it politely, took a sip and looked at her like a confused child. He wanted to believe in miracles but his age wouldn't allow it. He kept walking with the cup in hand.

'Would you like to have something for a snack?' she inquired from the kitchen and started foraging through the snack drawers.

'Tea would be just fine for now,' he said and kept on pacing while drinking the herbal tea in a leisurely mood. As the noises coming from outside were deafening, he went on to close the windows and switched on the air-conditioning as well.

Parvati BK was already seated on the sofa by now and she had served herself three choices of her favourite snack: bhujia, chewra and daalmoth, which were conveniently placed on the coffee table.

'Please have some,' she invited him, but he failed to notice and his pacing did not stop. She grabbed a film magazine from the coffee table and flipped through the pages while enjoying the snacks. Parvati was emitting some chewing noises as she savoured the crispy snacks and he wondered how she could eat them with herbal tea. She responded with an innocent childlike smile.

Just then his mobile phone rang. He placed the teacup on the coffee table and answered. 'Raiji, how are things lately?' After a pause, he said, 'I am fine, thank you. That is great, what date was that? Coming Friday! No problem at all. How many people? Around twenty-two, that is great. Yes, do you have anything particular that we should prepare? No, no, it is no hassle. The usual ones are fine. Yes, we have everything and it won't be a problem at all. Oh, thank you, thank you! What time will you be arriving then – 7 to 8 p.m. will be perfectly fine. No worries, I will make all the arrangements. It is confirmed, right? Okay, okay, thank you. No, no, you don't need any deposit. We have known each other for so long and that won't be a necessity. Don't mention it. Pukka! Okay? Confirmed? Thank you so much, we'll see you this Friday then, bye-bye!'

The reaction and excitement that he had displayed during the conversation clearly suggested that he was really happy. She didn't have to ask anything.

'Finally there is some good news,' he declared with a glowing smile as he sat opposite her on the sofa. The boredom as well as the restlessness was all gone for good.

'That is very good news! Who was that?' she asked with excitement and acted like she hadn't heard anything at all.

'Oh, that was Gobardhan Rai, he is an ex from 7 GR and lives in Kennedy Town,' he replied with a twinkle.

'What is the occasion? They sounded quite excited,' she teased him.

'It is a Numbaries gathering, an army word for intake: those who joined the army in the same batch of a certain year,' he explained as an army veteran who knew a few things.

'Oh, that's great!' she said supportively as she joined in his happiness. 'Twenty-two is quite a big crowd and hope we have enough time for preparation.'

'Don't worry, we have served even bigger crowds before,' he assured her. 'Our friends from Dharan can drink. We need to restock more drinks though.'

'We might have to inform our regular customers as well in advance,' she reminded him.

'That's easy, I will put up a notice on the door soon.' He already had it planned.

'Army guys are certainly a loud bunch, we have to be careful so we don't upset our neighbours.' She sounded as cautious as she had always been.

'Don't worry, Wan Chai has never been a quiet place anyway.'

He wasn't worried. He got up, walked to the kitchen and added more hot water to his cup. Then, he came back with the kettle and helped fill up her teacup as well.

All he needed to settle down for the afternoon was one piece of good news, and an early reservation of twenty-two people at the restaurant was a lot more than he needed. He was certainly going to have a nice relaxing afternoon for sure. Before too long, he was already ensconced on the comfy sofa with tea in one hand and the TV remote in the other and had started flipping the channels around as if he had no worries in the world.

Noticing the change on his face, she could make out that he was very happy. She didn't utter a word and tacitly kept on perusing the magazine she had been looking at for a while.

'Did Michael tell you what he was doing on a Sunday afternoon?' he suddenly asked as he began channel surfing.

'He is visiting an elderly home on the Kowloon side and fixing rooms,' she said with pride as if he were doing something great and noble for society.

'Instead of public service, he should concentrate more on his future and find some real work,' her husband expressed displeasure at his son's way of having an ideal job.

'He still has plenty of time to think about the future,' she defended her son as all mothers do. 'Besides, he doesn't need to find another job, he already has one at home and he has to take over the restaurant sooner or later.'

'That's fine. But he should also try to gain some experience outside before taking over the restaurant job, and I think it is time we should start looking for a nice girl so he can be married and settle down soon.' He couldn't hide his excitement. It was this fatherly wish he had been harbouring since the birth of his son and it was yet to be fulfilled.

'I agree but the new generations think differently. As the elders used to say, everything should fall into place when the timing is right and perhaps it is not the right time yet.' She sounded rather philosophical but which parents don't? After all, they were talking about the most important event of their life – their children's marriage.

'But everything comes with an expiry date and so does our patience,' he complained. 'I think we have to start talking with him soon.'

'I couldn't agree more.' She was well aware of the urgency of the discussion and knew they had to start talking soon.

'What is Donna up to lately? She didn't even get to rest on Sunday?' Now he had turned to the daughter and wanted to know if all was fine.

'She went to the convention centre with her friends. Don't you remember? We were both here when she told us at the same time. Sympo…symposium or something like that. She said she was going to attend and it was about work,' his wife explained in great detail.

'I wasn't paying attention, I suppose,' he said and added more water to the cup. 'I think we should also start looking for a nice young man and marry her off soon. After all, she is a girl and we should follow our tradition before society starts talking.'

'I know, both of our children are getting older,' she lamented. 'Regardless of boy or girl, we should start talking about it. But I am afraid they won't heed our suggestions that easily, and I am a little bit concerned. Especially since both of our children are quite independent and strong-minded.'

'Of course, we cannot force them,' he said seriously. 'Our job as parents is to provide good guidance, give them a choice and the final decision will have to be their own. After all, marriage is a very important decision in our lives and we cannot impose ours upon them. They must have full consent on the final decision.'

'Yes, you are absolutely right. It is not like our time and they won't accept what they were told as we did. Like you said, we can suggest, provide guidance and let them make the final decision,' she agreed.

'Let's start talking about it in front of the children. They are old enough to understand the marriage issue and we shouldn't feel embarrassed talking about it. At the same time, I will have a look around at my side of the family and you also do the same on your side. Once we have found something concrete, we will first discuss it between us and only then will we tell them. That will be the best way to handle this sensitive issue. What do you say?' he asked, his eyes sparkling and she instantly agreed.

It was a very significant decision and they were genuinely pleased that they got to do that together as a responsible couple. The future of their children was surely in two safe pairs of hands. They said to each other and anticipated a bright future.

It was already late afternoon by then and he started flipping the TV channels again before settling down for the local news channel. It was mostly broadcasting local news, and it must have been a very long time since he had watched any.

A taxi driver was busted for overcharging; demonstrators of all types asked for compensation from the government; a drunk foreigner was caught groping a woman at Lan Kwai Fong; politicians were squabbling and bickering on similar issues as usual; pundits were commenting on expensive house prices and the stock market; commentators blamed and trashed mainlanders for almost everything in Hong Kong; a pedestrian was knocked down by a Porsche; a few more cases involving domestic helpers and their unscrupulous agents; news about the Tourism Board's increasing woes as the number of visitors dwindled; a truck, while reversing, injured an elderly man; and so on. Such news had become so common nowadays in Hong Kong that they were hardly missed. There was nothing new, and he suddenly felt like he hadn't missed anything at all since the last session of the news.

Then the last piece of news suddenly caught his attention. A three-year-old boy had fallen from the window of a third-floor apartment building in Jordan. The boy sustained only a few minor injuries and survived the ordeal. The parents said to be of Nepalese origin were arrested and taken to the nearby Yau Ma Tei police station for questioning. No charges of negligence were yet to be announced by the police.

'Not again…!' he said out loud in sheer frustration and dismay. He had already stood up and was holding his head by both hands. 'How could they let such terrible things happen? Why don't our people understand it? We don't live in the village anymore. When will we learn? The parents' negligence and stupidity could have ended the child's life. What were they thinking? It's so horrible! Why is it only happening to our community? It is not only terrible but also embarrassing. The locals must think that we are jungle people. Most importantly, the child could have been crippled or even dead. Just unbelievable!'

'We live here in Hong Kong but our mentality is like we are still in Nepal. It never changes. Unless we change that, nothing is going to happen,' his wife added. Despite her humble beginning, she was a learned lady and understood life very well. She couldn't have said it better and what she heard surprised her as well.

'Exactly!' He agreed. 'How many innocent children must die before we realize that? The problem with our people is that we don't do things properly and we don't listen to others. Nobody wants to be told anything. No wonder we are still so backward.' He let out his frustration once and for all.

'Please calm down. I know you are absolutely right but please don't say that in public' she answered. 'You know how our people are. They don't think twice before using force and harming others. We should stay out of it and avoid unnecessary headaches,' she reminded him and he knew she was right. There was no point worrying about it anymore and he knew he had to calm down. The sun was about to go down soon and the lights on the nearby buildings and streets were gradually coming to life.

Chapter 12

It had already been three weeks since they had last met and today's gathering brought new excitement to all. The hot weather was certainly a nuisance and sitting under the tin roof without air-conditioning for a long time was definitely not fun. Nevertheless, it didn't dampen their mood and everyone was looking forward to it.

It was late Saturday afternoon. All four friends of the Namaste Club had already arrived and were busy preparing the special meal for tonight. Due to the hot temperature, everyone was forced to shed their outer clothes and wear only vests and shorts. The place had only one pedestal fan and it was put on the highest spin possible.

'It must be over thirty-five degrees Celsius today. It is really hot,' Krishna Sharma said with a grimace while he swiped his brows with the back of his right hand.

'I think it is too hot for cooking. Let's wait for the temperature to go down a bit,' Manohar BK pointed out.

'Yes, it is just too damn hot. The tin roof doesn't help either,' Sher Bikram Thapa agreed.

'That's a good idea. Besides, we have plenty of time. Have more water,' Ram Bahadur Gurung said while passing the water bottle to the others.

'By looking at ourselves just now, our old days in the army came flashing back,' Sher Bikram Thapa said with a nostalgic look and the others looked towards him.

'Yes, it was just like yesterday. We had to work in both rain and heat. No excuses,' Ram Bahadur Gurung added as he remembered the good old days when he was in the army.

'As I have never been in the army, I have no experience, but they say army life is tough and strict,' Krishna Sharma pitched in. He was curious to know more.

'It certainly is,' Sher Bikram Thapa confirmed. 'We had a few experiences every year and everyone from the whole garrison stationed in Hong Kong had to participate. It was mostly a week-long exercise and each battalion started from a different part of Hong Kong. Some started from Sai Kung or Plover Cove; some others started from Tai Lam or Castle Peak areas. But the exercise always ended on Lantau Island. The day would start with the digging of trenches, and we were only allowed to take our shirts off. By the end of the day, our backs got so terribly burnt that our skins were either charred or peeled off like roasted meat. After seeing our own condition here, I remembered those old days and couldn't hold myself back.'

'We didn't even get to rest at night.' It was Ram Bahadur Gurung's turn to get emotional and carry on from where his friend had left off. 'There was night patrol, sentry duty as well as sporadic harassment from the enemy side. Base camp had to be changed every two days and a new camp had to be secured. Our main task during the day was digging and all the marching was done in the veil of darkness at night.'

'So, by the time it ended, you must have marched for at least a hundred miles or more, right?' Krishna Sharma had guessed correctly. He and Manohar BK, who were the civilians of the group, were fascinated by the story and wanted to know each and every detail related to it.

'Yes, almost everyone had blisters on their hands and feet,' Sher Bikram Thapa said, as if it were some sort of symbol of valour or achievement.

'We were not even allowed to take our boots off, let alone change clothes or socks. We either got soaked in the rain or baked a hundred times in the heat. Order was order. You don't talk back in the army. By the end of the exercise, the barracks were filled up with mephitic smells and needed thorough cleaning before the foul smells could go away. Many also suffered from body rashes and skin disorders. But nobody escaped from Hong Kong Foot and we are suffering from it even now.' Ram Bahadur Gurung concluded the story with light banter that everybody in Hong Kong knew about. Hong Kong Foot is a chronic foul-smelling foot disease.

'That is the reason why most of the ex-Gurkha soldiers have Hong Kong Foot,' Manohar BK said in a joking tone and everybody had a good laugh.

'It means there are no country parks in Hong Kong you guys have not walked on,' Krishna Sharma said and it was nothing but the truth.

'We probably know more about Hong Kong's country parks than the streets.' Ram Bahadur Gurung confirmed with a sense of pride.

'What about the food? Did you guys cook by yourself or got food delivered?' Krishna Sharma asked with an impish look and waited impatiently.

'We used to have a standard ration pack,' Sher Bikram Thapa said with a smile. 'It had rice, mutton, ghee, lentils, biscuits and other necessary stuff to cook a decent meal. But it was quite heavy and took a longer time to cook. It also came with a pack of burning wax and a portable stove. As we had to carry weapons, ammunition and other stuff in the army pack, adding ration packs didn't help at all, and we had to find a solution. Then, we found noodles, and everybody started carrying packed noodles with canned ham, sardines and anchovies instead of the ration pack, and our problem was solved once and for all. Noodles were easy to cook, hence very convenient.'

'Almost everyone had ration packs in their cupboard and it created another problem during the time of inspection. We had to hide them somewhere so the inspecting officer wouldn't find it and demand an explanation,' Ram Bahadur Gurung explained.

'Yes, it was tough but also memorable,' Sher Bikram Thapa exclaimed.

I don't think we can understand, let alone appreciate it,' Manohar BK said. He knew there was a big difference between the life of an ex-army guy and civilians like him.

'It was not only a sense of discipline, duty and tenacity but also camaraderie and loyalty as well as gratefulness that the army taught you, and that is precisely what civilians like us lack to a great extent.' Krishna Sharma said. 'Gurkha is a name that commands respect throughout the world. But there is a big difference between earning it by being one and gaining it by heredity, and you won't understand it unless you have gone through it. We have learned a lot from you two, but we still lack the full understanding of its greatness and that's what makes us all different. Imagine a guy who had never heard or met a Gurkha before. It would be extremely hard for them to comprehend without any prior knowledge, and we cannot blame them.'

'But it is very important that we know about it. Because without them, we wouldn't even be here, right?' Manohar BK couldn't agree more.

'Sadly, our people never seemed to realize this fact,' Ram

Bahadur Gurung lamented. 'Being selfish and ungrateful is in our blood.'

'We have learnt this from each other,' Manohar BK added with a sigh of hopelessness.

'What happened to our people? If we continue like this, we are done!' Sher Bikram Thapa said with firm conviction.

'No wonder the situation of our country is so bad.' Manohar BK took another sigh.

'Not everything is doomed yet, we still have some hope and we should always remain positive.' Krishna Sharma was still in a rallying mood.

'Had it not been for our situation, we wouldn't even be here in the first place and that says it all,' Ram Bahadur Gurung said with a firm voice and the conversation came to an end. There was nothing left to be said again, hence a long silence prevailed.

The scorching sun had already started coming down and the heat was becoming bearable. A huge thick cloud appeared out of nowhere and blocked the sun for good. It was time to start the cooking job again.

'Chopping is my department, so, please don't bother,' Krishna Sharma declared and started hoarding things, which needed cutting before the cooking. Tonight's special was the traditional Nepalese dish called Sukuti and Gundruk. 'How should I cut them? Like this one?' He showed one small cut piece of dried meat to Manohar BK for approval and continued the rest once his friend nodded back.

'Are you paying any attention to the situation of those drug addicts? People seemed to talk a lot about them these days, including the media and I think it is a terrible situation to be in. Hope somebody will help them.' Ram Bahadur Gurung had suddenly begun a new topic and everybody became attentive. It had been in the news for a while now.

'I really don't understand why they take drugs in the first place,' Sher Bikram Thapa pitched in. 'Whichever way we look at it, Hong Kong is a hundred times better than what we have back in Nepal, and I genuinely don't know why they would waste such a great opportunity by taking drugs. Unbelievable!'

'I think it is a bit of everything, like a cocktail,' Manohar BK ventured. He was a restaurateur and he would know his drink. 'It can be from anything, including language, culture, loneliness, peer-effect, insecurity, disappointment, separation, betrayal, weak mentality, homesickness, culture shock, depression, failure and so on. Most importantly, they failed to assimilate into the society, succumbed to desperation and the problem got the better of them. All in all, it is a terrible thing and they should get out of it as soon as possible. Sadly it is easier said than done.'

'Our so-called community leaders are too busy blowing their own trumpet, the locals see us as nothing more than trouble, and the government is too busy placating the expectations of people and ingratiating themselves for Beijing's favour,' Krishna Sharma said while preparing the materials for the evening meal. 'Nobody is coming to help, and they should either find a way out or die a horrible death.'

'It is such a pity that we could do nothing about it,' Ram Bahadur Gurung sighed. 'Our Nepalese community in Hong Kong is so divided that there is nothing much we can do about it. What's more, we are only good at talking, and when it is time for action, nobody steps forward.'

'What is in it for me? Our selfish culture asks and stops us from doing anything at all,' Manohar BK pitched in.

'We do nothing unless there are personal gains,' Krishna Sharma added.

'Those with power won't act and those with heart have no power.' Sher Bikram Thapa sounded philosophical.

'That's why our country is still in such a dire situation.' Ram Bahadur Gurung summarized the ongoing discussion in a single sentence. There was nothing left for the others to add, and there was a comfortable silence for a while.

The final cooking started with a big noise, rice was almost cooked and the evening lights were switched on in the nearby premises and streets. Manohar BK got busy with the cooking, Sher Bikram Thapa prepared the plates, Krishna Sharma cleared the used stuff as well as garbage, and Ram Bahadur Gurung got himself busy by rearranging the seating for all four. When the special meal was finally ready and served, it was precisely 7.30 p.m. Not much was spoken during the meal.

By the time the special meal was over and washing up was done, it was almost 8.30 p.m. and the happy and satiated bunch took their positions on the floor, albeit in a relaxed mood. All the foods and beverages that they had brought had been consumed by now except the last round of drinks, which they would take right before their departure. It was mostly a mixture of canned beer, soft drinks and juice.

'It seems that our people are unexpectedly dying lately,' Sher Bikram Thapa initiated a new topic while taking a small sip from the beer can. 'They came back from work, had dinner and went to sleep without any complaints whatsoever. The next morning, they are gone. The mysterious death puzzled all.'

'It seems like an ongoing trend. I have also heard about such incidents,' Manohar BK added.

'Yes, it is quite alarming for all,' Ram Bahadur Gurung said in a sad tone.

'I think it might be a stroke, heart failure, or something

related to other chronic diseases,' Krishna Sharma maintained. 'We know how careless people are, we have a tendency of not seeking medical assistance until we faint or can't move, and by the time we find out, it is already too late. Furthermore, we don't control our diet, we take anything we like and that is an extremely dangerous habit. We play with our health and don't even realize it. I am sure that it might be one of those reasons why we are facing so many unexpected deaths in our community today, and it is sad because it is avoidable. All we need is a little bit of knowledge about health, regularly exercise and try to live a healthy life.'

'You are absolutely right. Our people are so busy making money that we never have time to think about other things like family, health, education, career, and so on in life and end up paying dearly with our own lives,' Ram Bahadur Gurung lamented.

'Understandably, without a job here in Hong Kong, life will be hard for all of us. But if you chart your life path properly, it can be managed with well-paid jobs that don't require such hardship, and we can still enjoy life in Hong Kong. Jobs are necessary but not something that should force you to neglect other important things in life. This is where we are failing as a community and making serious mistakes,' Manohar BK pitched in. He had a good point.

'Everybody is after money in Hong Kong, especially our people. We have to think not only about our living here in Hong Kong, but also back in Nepal as well, and that is where the main problem lies,' Sher Bikram Thapa said. He had indeed nailed it.

'No matter what, we must show off,' Krishna Sharma added.

'Must build bigger and taller houses than thy neighbour,' Ram Bahadur Gurung said.

'Flaunting wealth is in our blood. Whether there is life or not, the race must go on and everybody has to run so that nobody is left behind,' Manohar BK said, sarcasm dripping.

Make your neighbour green with envy. Create such an illusion within the society back in Nepal that life is good as gold abroad and money actually grows on trees. But in reality, our people work as coolies. When they die, no one is bothered. In the pursuit of impressing people who won't even matter in their lives, they forget more important things that might make a difference in their own lives.

When the four friends locked up the door behind them and finally left the place, it was already 10 p.m. As they said their goodbyes and headed home, they were already thinking about the next meeting. However, what they didn't know was that this was the last meeting they would have in this place and that they were never coming back here again. Whether it was for the good or bad, only time would tell.

Chapter 13

It had been persistently raining for the whole week and working outdoors was getting extremely difficult. People living in shoeboxes like apartments in Hong Kong, had their own dilemmas: especially the nuisance of drying clothes. Life was already tough for people and the non-stop rain didn't help at all. The construction industry got hit hard. The sites were muddy, slippery and full of potholes. Working on tall buildings and underground became riskier and accidents were unavoidable. The Nepalese community wasn't spared from this ordeal since they were an integral part of the construction industry and many were injured and lost their lives. Sher Bikram Thapa was one of the unfortunate ones and had been nursing the wound on his hand at Queen Elizabeth Hospital, Kowloon. It had already been two weeks since the accident and his old friends from the Namaste Club were finally visiting him one evening.

It was a general in-patient ward with twelve beds, six on each side. He had a side table on the right side of the bed and a movable desk on the front of it that could be used as a dinner table as well. Sher Bikram Thapa's bed was the first bed on the right from the main entrance. His right hand was still in a plaster. When his friends had finally arrived, he was resting on his back and welcomed them with a smile. He tried to sit up straight.

'So much happened and you didn't think it important to

inform us…?' Ram Bahadur Gurung said with a grimace and stood next to the bed.

'Exactly! If we had not contacted you, we wouldn't even have come to know about it,' Krishna Sharma added as he stood on the other side of the bed.

'We would have come earlier if we had known,' Manohar BK said as he leaned over the front desk. He had carried the fruit basket on behalf of the three visiting friends and had placed it on Sher's desk.

'Sorry, I cannot move. There are some stools over there, please help yourself,' he told them since he hadn't heard what the friends were saying. Manohar BK, who was closest to the stools, walked over and returned with three stools. They positioned themselves around the bed and sat on the stools before the conversation resumed.

'What happened?' the three friends asked almost at the same time.

'It was raining heavily,' Sher Bikram Thapa finally opened up. But his face clearly showed the affliction he was experiencing. The memory alone must have been really painful for him, but it needed to be told for his own sake as well as for his friends. 'I was working at the tunnel entrance, moving things here and there and tidying up the place in order to avoid flooding. That is when we found a heavy metal panel on the floor. It was in the way and had to be removed. I tried to move it on my own but couldn't since it was very heavy. One of my co-workers came to help. We held it with our hands from both ends and, lifting it, tried to slowly move it to the corner. The ground was full of floodwater as high as our shins and we didn't see the actual ground as we walked. There happened to be a big pothole on the way. I was walking backward while carrying the load, and fell into it. I lost my balance and fell on the right side. Unfortunately, the metal panel, which had slipped from our hands, dropped on my right hand. What's more, the floor on which my hand landed was on top of a boulder and my hand got crushed between the metal panel and the boulder. My co-worker tried to hold the panel up on his own but failed and slipped and lost his balance. I didn't realize what had happened, but I was suddenly hit by such excruciating pain that I fainted. When I regained conscious, I found myself here. An emergency surgery was conducted to save my mangled fingers. Three fingers – index, middle and third – were severely crushed. But they could only save two and my index finger had to be amputated. It was a bad day and I am here now.'

'Sorry to hear that. It must be really painful even now,' Ram Bahadur Gurung said.

'Yes, the pain was just unbearable. You don't know about such things until it happens to you and it would be impossible without painkillers. I still have to take painkillers three times a day and it is still quite painful,' Sher Bikram Thapa said. His friends could only imagine what he had been through.

'When does the cast come off?' Krishna Sharma inquired.

'At least a few more weeks, the doctor hasn't decided yet,' Sher replied.

'Do you feel something different in there?' Manohar BK sounded curious.

'I can still feel it but nothing stranger than before. I haven't seen it yet and don't know what to expect when it is finally taken off.' He replied with an innocent look and felt the outside of the plaster cast with his left hand.

'I don't think we can even comprehend the pain you were experiencing then. How do you feel now?' Ram Bahadur Thapa was concerned.

'I don't know how to explain, but it is more or less like

numbing after periodic shudders of excruciating pain, and it won't go away until I take the painkiller. But nowadays, it is a lot better and I can stand it. It was simply unbearable in the beginning, and I had to be sedated by the painkiller all the time.' The memory of that difficult experience alone made him sweat and he was finding it difficult to continue talking.

'Hope there is no need for another surgery again,' Manohar BK said.

'I don't think so. The first one was successful,' he said with a slight smile.

'Thank God, all went well.' Krishna Sharma sighed and added, 'Hope it won't be too long before you can go home. Is it decided yet?'

'Not sure, maybe within a few weeks' time I will be allowed to go home,' he said, eyes twinkling. 'Home' was the word that made him happy and hopeful.

'You have been in such a critical situation and you still didn't inform us. You know we are friends, right?' Manohar BK wasn't done with him yet and he complained.

'The answer is already in your own question. You already said we are friends. That's why! The last thing I wanted to see was you guys with sad faces,' he said with sincerity.

'Anyway, we are here now. Please don't hesitate to ask if we can be of any help in any way. Seriously, guys, we are friends. That's why we are here for you. Please always keep that in mind,' Ram Bahadur Gurung said on everyone's behalf and they all nodded in sync to show their support and solidarity.

'Thank you so much. I am genuinely honoured,' Sher Bikram said and his chest expanded with pride. 'I know you guys are for real and I wasn't expecting anything less than that. But I am okay, please don't worry about me, I will be just fine.'

'Are you sure? You don't have to feel sorry or uncomfortable with us. We really mean it and you already know that.' Krishna Sharma wanted to make sure that all of his friends were with him and fully understood it.

'I am good. I know you guys really care for me and I am grateful. Thank you so much. No worries!' He was not only trying to convince them but also brimming with pride all at the same time. If you are lucky enough to have such good friends, who wouldn't?

'Okay, we will accept your explanation on one condition,' Manohar BK looked at the other two friends. 'You must promise us that whenever you face a problem, you will not only share it with us immediately, but also let us help you without refusing.

'And the offer is not only for you but also for us all. If it is your turn today, it can be mine tomorrow, and he will be next. So there is nothing to be worried about.' It was Ram Bahadur Sharma who pitched in and settled the case once and for all.

'Okay, okay, I promise! I will hide nothing from you all henceforth. Happy?' He finally accepted the offer with humility and needless to say, it pleased everyone.

'How long do you think it will take for the wound to heal? Did the doctor say anything?' Krishna Sharma asked. He was concerned about the recovery.

'The doctor said it depends from patient to patient. It will take at least a half to one whole year. But I don't think I will ever be working again in the construction field,' he said with an expressionless face. He didn't know whether to appear happy or sad.

'What do you have in mind then as an alternative?' Manohar BK was curious.

'Security guard, what else can we do?' he replied in a jiffy.

'Maybe we can work together in the future!' Ram Bahadur Gurung joked.

'What about the hospital expenses? Hope your company is paying for it,' Krishna Sharma enthused.

'The expense here is not much as it is a government hospital. Our company has agreed to keep on paying while I am in recovery, and everything has been taken care of,' he said with a grateful look. He knew his friends were genuinely concerned.

'What about the insurance? They certainly must have an insurance policy for all workers as it is required by law in Hong Kong, and you should start the claiming procedure soon.' This came from Krishna Sharma and he wanted to help his friend in need.

'That one I haven't started yet. I am also not sure of how this thing works. I have heard people say that I need to hire a lawyer, and I don't even know where to find one,' he said in confusion and waited for the others to speak out.

'Don't worry! Our friend here can help arrange everything for you, right?' Ram Bahadur Gurung said with a broad smile. He was talking about Krishna Sharma who had all the necessary knowledge on such issues.

'Absolutely, he is the best in Hong Kong and just assume that it is already done. What are friends for?' Manohar BK said.

'Sorry for the trouble, friend. I am totally relying on you then.' He had no choice but to accept the offer and be grateful.

'Don't say that.' Krishna Sharma waved his hand like an artist's brush. 'I will do my best to find the right lawyer and then I will inform you. Before that you have to send me all the necessary details including the name of the company, incident place, date, time, HKID card number, work ID, and so on. Then we will decide how to proceed further in the best possible way. Don't worry!'

'The best would be to arrange a meeting with you and the lawyer and talk over everything in detail,' Ram Bahadur Gurung duly suggested and Manohar BK agreed.

'That would be the second step of the process. First of all, you need to provide those details to me before I can talk with the lawyer and based on that material, he will make necessary plans, and you will have to confirm it personally before we lodge the case,' Krishna Sharma explained and the issue of handling the insurance policy was thus settled.

'Thank you, if it's okay, I can provide that information now,' he urged.

'Don't be in such a hurry. You can SMS them to me by tonight or tomorrow and then we will work it out together between us. Not a problem.' Krishna Sharma explained. 'We will just have to keep in touch all the time and that should be all.'

A duty nurse came in, did her regular check and moved to the next patient.

'What about the food here? Hospital food is definitely not that appetizing and we are not accustomed to having such bland dishes on a regular basis.' Manohar BK had started the conversation again after the duty nurse had moved on.

'Do you know everybody who has come to visit me asked the same question? But believe me or not, I don't feel like that as I never had any problems with any type of food in my life. I am okay with any food that is served to me. I can eat them and I don't have anything special that I want or don't want to eat,' he explained with ease, but his friends stared at him with a strange look.

It was also the reason behind their utter silence. Despite knowing him for so long, his friends were still unaware of this fact and that caught them by complete surprise.

'Still, you must be craving for a home-cooked meal though…!' Krishna Sharma waded in. He still couldn't bring himself into a position where he didn't long for typical Nepali food like daal, *bhaat* and *tarkari* with heavy gravies.

'I don't mean I don't crave them but I am not desperate. Whenever I am hungry and have food to eat, I am happy with it. I don't know why but it's me, so here I am.' He said it as easily as he had started and, with that last word, there was nothing left to say any more. He was indeed a man who could be made happy very easily.

'So you are planning to eat the hospital food as long as you are here, right?' Ram Bahadur Gurung inquired.

'Yes, I don't see any problem with that. I even told my wife not to burden herself by bringing food for me here in the hospital. Our place is quite far from here, as you all know, and I don't like to create unnecessary trouble,' he explained and his friends were impressed. What the ordinary guy said was in fact quite a big thing and carried great significance. The way it was said made it even more special. Yet, the greatest deal of the whole conversation was this – he wasn't even aware of what he had just said.

A group of new visitors consisting of two young women, a white man and a black man came in. They were Sher Bikram Thapa's two daughters and their new husbands. Realizing the crowded situation, the old friends said goodbye and left him in the safe hands of his new family. They promised to come back again. Coincidently, it also was the day when they were supposed to meet at their usual gathering place back at the rooftop and they had missed it for the very first time. What they didn't know yet was that it was just the beginning and they were never going to meet there again.

Chapter 14

The atmosphere was peaceful, most of the guests had left and only a few close family members had remained. The Gonpa, a Buddhist monastery, was located in a medium-sized flat in a high-rise building in Mong Kok. It had an open and spacious praying area and a small kitchen, a pantry and a bathroom. The front side at the farthest wall had a huge decorative display cabinet festooned with Lord Buddha in various sizes and shapes, colourful scriptures, as well as hangings, and a bell and a lamp. The centrepiece of the display was a giant golden Buddha statue adorned with a colourful scarf, flowers and offerings. The place also had many oil lamps, candles and incense.

The wall on the left side had nothing but a few portraits hanging on it. On the right side, which was the window side, had a seating place on an elevated platform for the chief monk. Next to him was the seating place for his two assistants, at floor level. In front of them was the wooden plank for reading books, a typical Lama's drum that came with a long wooden handle, and a big metal bell. The whole floor was fitted with many square wooden planks, and seating cushions were provided for worshippers.

It was the final day of the ongoing ritual: one hundred and eight burning lamps had been offered in respect of the departed soul, and the close members from the mourning family had duly gathered at the Gonpa. Once the ritual was over, the crowd, which had filled most of the room, gradually thinned out and only a few had remained.

'Maybe we should be moving by now, Baba!' Trimol Gurung, the younger son of Ram Bahadur Gurung, suggested as they prepared to return home. Next to him were his mother and Trimol's Chinese wife waiting to leave. Each of them had carried a canvas bag that was empty by now.

'What time is it?' Ram Bahadur Gurung asked. Absorbed in the ritual, he had lost track of time.

'Almost 3.30 p.m., Baba!' his son reminded him. The son waited for a while before repeating that it was time to go home.

'Oh, yes, yes!' Ram Bahadur Gurung said. Then he turned towards his family and said, 'Why don't you three go home first? I have some friends here and I need to catch up with them before I get back.' He pointed to a group of three men at the other corner who looked over fifty and were dressed completely in black. They acknowledged him with a faint smile as his family looked over at them.

'Okay Baba, we will make a move then. Take care!' his son said and started moving. Ram's Chinese daughter-in-law murmured and waved goodbye before heading towards the door.

'Don't be late, ha!' his wife said and followed the other two. Ram followed them to the door. Then she stopped as she remembered something important, turned and asked, 'Will you be home in time for dinner?' He didn't say anything in response, but raised his right hand to his face and dropped it instantaneously as if to say 'Don't worry, it is not a big deal and now just go home.'

Once the family had left, he walked over to his friends and suggested they have a seat in the pantry, which had a small table and four metal folding chairs. They each grabbed a seat and sat there. The assistant at the Gonpa offered them green tea and they drank with melancholy faces as they searched for the right words to start a new conversation.

'You guys don't have to worry about me. I will be just fine and thank you so much for coming here today.' Ram Bahadur Gurung was aware of what his friends were going through, he couldn't make them uncomfortable and started the conversation.

'What happened? I know it is painful to repeat the same story but I believe sharing can lessen the pain and we are here to share,' Krishna Sharma, the most talkative member of the group asked. He was certainly talking for the whole group.

'It is karma, I suppose,' Ram Bahadur Gurung said with a sigh. 'But to be honest, the moment we realized our son had ASD (autism spectrum disorder), I knew destiny had already betrayed him. There was no turning back. It was just the matter of when, but not if or why. I knew it was a done deal and knowingly or unknowingly, I was somehow preparing myself for the worst. I didn't know it was meant to be that way or that soon. Perhaps it was karma, we don't get what we wish for, and whatever was supposed to happen, will happen anyway. And my son's position was no different.'

'We are just a small part of His great plan.' Manohar BK became philosophical. The array of recent events in their lives had made everyone sensible, and ordinary guys like them started talking like intellectuals. 'We still wanted to hear what had actually happened. The accident occurred in the bathroom, right? What happened?' Needless to say, the focus of the three friends was firmly on Ram Bahadur Gurung.

'It was a Friday afternoon, he was to take a shower and his mom was making the preparations, as usual.' Ram Bahadur Gurung started with a soft voice and sipped a mouthful of green tea before starting again. 'Surprisingly, he had been insisting on doing it on his own. It was the very first time he was to take a shower by himself. It certainly surprised his mother, and she tried to explain to him that it wasn't a good idea. I wasn't at home at that fateful moment. But he said such sweet things like he was already a grown-up man, he was embarrassed, and he should start learning how to take care of himself henceforth. She thought he was absolutely right. Besides, what could go wrong anyway? After all, he was only taking a shower in his own home, right?'

'He was very happy and they even had a great laugh as he pushed her out of the bathroom. As he locked the door from the inside and started the shower, she didn't think much about it and went back to the kitchen. About five minutes later, there was a thumping sound from the bathroom as if something big had dropped on the floor and a horrible howling sound followed. My startled wife ran towards the bathroom. She called his name first, knocked on the door and waited anxiously for an answer. But he didn't respond. She kept on banging the door in panic but still no reply. She tried to force open the door but couldn't do so on her own. Then she called me and cried out for me to return home in a hurry. In desperation, she banged on our neighbour's door, cried out for help, and it was the neighbour who helped break open the bathroom door. What she saw in the shower was the worst nightmare any mother could bear to see. Her own child was unconscious with a bloodied head and there was blood all over.'

Ram couldn't continue and started sobbing. There was complete silence. Everyone remained quiet until he was ready to speak again.

'It took me almost twenty minutes before I could get home,' Ram Bahadur Gurung continued with a trembling voice. 'By the time I reached home, it was already too late, and both police and an ambulance had already arrived. It was like a scene in a movie. He was wrapped up and, on a stretcher, ready to be taken to the hospital, and his mother had passed out. She was not in a position to talk. The only difference between the movie and my situation was that they were my loved ones and nobody was playing a role and everything was for real. What's more, unlike in a movie, there was no sad music playing in the background. I was not only alone, but it had scared the hell out of me as my world came crashing down. The experience was just horrible. So much so that you don't even want your worst enemy to go through that horror. It was beyond our imagination.'

'I know what you mean. I have been through that pain and survived. Although mine was physical and yours was mental, they both invoked the same result,' Sher Bikram Thapa spoke for the very first time since they had been seated there. The notion alone made him shudder, and he could feel the same old pain all over his body from his hand injury. Like Ram, they were experiences that lasted for a lifetime.

'By the time he arrived at the hospital,' Ram continued, 'it was already too late and all the power of the modern world couldn't save him. The tile floor of the shower was slippery from the shampoo mixed with water. When he dropped the soap bar during his shower and tried to pick it up again, he accidently stepped onto it, slipped, and took a big fall. During the fall, his head got caught on the sharp edge of the granite and sustained a huge cut resulting in a broken skull and damaged brain. Even an emergency surgery couldn't save his life. He hung on for the next two days but eventually gave up on the third day. Our dear son was gone, and there was nothing we could do to save him.' Tears started rolling down his face and the silent sobbing continued.

'I know, no matter what we say or do, we won't be able to make up for your loss. But grief is such an aspect of our life that we all have to face it sometime and the only way to wrestle with grief is by sharing it with others. I know it is hard for old men like us to cry openly, but someone has to do it anyway and why not here with us? Let's cry together, pray together for the departed soul and hope for the soul to rest in peace.' Krishna Sharma led the pack with his example and the remaining friends followed suit. 'Let the angels take him under their wing and bring him to God and let's be grateful for that,' Manohar BK continued like he was reciting from a scripture.

'He is happy with him up there now, there is nothing to worry now, and I know he will protect us from all the bad omens,' Sher Bikram Thapa added.

They mourned together in silence for some time.

'Despite your situation, you have come and I can't thank you enough. Especially you, my friend, hope you are recovering well.' The last bit was for Sher Bikram Thapa. Ram Bahadur Gurung became emotional, but he was genuinely happy and grateful that his friends were here.

'It is a lot better now but I still have to wear those supportive gears and take a painkiller. However, I just take them when it really hurts, and I have to go for therapy on a weekly basis. I suppose it will be a long time before I can fully recover and they said the pain will come back, especially in winter, which means it is here to stay,' Sher Bikram Thapa explained in great detail. It sounded like he had accepted the situation that fate had bestowed upon him. He was prepared.

'Did you sort out the insurance issue?' Despite his anguish, Ram Bahadur Gurung was still concerned about his friend and he couldn't hold himself back.

'It is already done and under process now. It should be fine, but don't worry. It is not the time to talk about it,' Krishna Sharma butted in. He didn't want his tired friend to end up with more stress. 'As far as I know, this should be the last ritual for your dear son, right? If there are still more, please let us know and we are here to pitch in.'

'Today was the last one. From now on, we will arrange a monthly visit to the Gonpa or other temple and offer flowers, candles and incense. Please don't worry and thank you so much,' Ram Bahadur Gurung replied. It had already been a fortnight since the departure of his son and the mourning was officially over with today's ritual.

'Is it okay for us to stay here for some more time? Hope the Gonpa staff won't mind. If not, maybe we should go out and find a place where we can stay and talk more,' Manohar BK suggested.

Although the Gonpa staff had no problem with them staying put, they eventually decided to leave. After expressing their gratitude and thanking the Gonpa officials, they left the place and went to a nearby fast-food restaurant where they could eat and drink while still engaging in conversation. Nobody wanted to return home yet.

The eatery was nearly empty, with only a few customers. They found nice quiet seats in the corner and sat there before ordering. The set menu for the dinner was not available yet so they had to wait.

'There is still some time before we can order. The afternoon tea menu is still on though. Shall we take something for now?' Krishna Sharma asked as they sat and looked at each other for comments.

'What is there to eat?' Sher Bikram Thapa enthused. He was always ready for treats.

'The usual, what else! As you know, they always carry the same stuff,' Manohar BK said as a regular who knew what food was served here.

'I don't feel like eating anything. Please help yourself. And just get me a cup of milk tea, thank you,' Ram Bahadur Gurung said in a soft voice.

'No, it cannot be, you must eat something,' Krishna Sharma insisted in a brotherly manner and tried to convince him.

After a quick discussion, Manohar BK and Sher Bikram Thapa went to check out the menu first, and returned with some recommendations. Then all three went to make the final order while Ram Bahadur Gurung remained seated. The new menu had already changed by now and it took just a couple of minutes before the ordered meals were served. The fast-food restaurants in Hong Kong are really quick and efficient, everything is readymade, and delivery is fast. What's more, the food is good, hot and hygienic too. Before too long, they all returned with the food of their choice and started talking as they ate. Their meal mostly consisted of rice, vegetables and meat with a drink.

'Since you don't want to eat meat, we have brought fruit salad and milk tea for you. Please have it,' Manohar BK urged as he passed the plate over to Ram Bahadur Gurung.

'Thank you!' Ram Bahadur Gurung accepted the food with humility. He knew his friends would not let him go without eating.

For the next twenty minutes, nobody said a word and ate until there was nothing left on the plates. After the most important ritual of their lives was completed, they leaned back on their chairs and made themselves comfortable with a drink. They had all ordered a cup of hot milk tea, an after-meal drink and took their time to savour it.

'It is certainly a difficult time for all. We must get a grip on ourselves and hope the family is coping well,' Krishna Sharma started with a light sip from his cup.

'How is our sister-in-law doing? She must be devastated,' Manohar BK expressed sympathy as he wiped his mouth with a tissue.

'She is a strong woman. She won't show it outside, but I am sure that she has cracked a thousand times inside. After all, he was our own flesh and blood.' Ram Bahadur Gurung said slowly.

'What's more, he was a grown-up and that would have made the suffering even harder,' Sher Bikram Thapa concluded the sentence that his friend had left unfinished.

'Sometimes, fate is really cruel. After all those years of togetherness and attachments, it is suddenly there no more, and the only thing left is sorrow for a lifetime.' Krishna Sharma became emotional and his words made others sad as well.

'Losing a child must be one of the greatest sorrows of our lives, no parent ever wants to live with such a burden and we were no exception.' Ram Bahadur Gurung finally opened up and the pain started flowing from his welled-up soul as words. 'And yet, we somehow found a reason to console our heart and accept it as an event that was meant to happen that way. Perhaps it was a way out for him, given the situation he was in, and he needed a break and his passing away was a salvation. The sorrow of losing him will always be there for us but this way, we don't have to worry about him anymore. Perhaps it was a good deal for him and us as well. If this makes us feel better, we even promised not to cry for him again. We will try to live a normal life from here on and that was the least we could do for him. We have no grievances with fate, God or anyone. We have already accepted this fact and learned to live with it as we wait for our turn to meet him again.'

'I think that is probably the most sensible thing I have ever heard.' Krishna Sharma said, breaking the silence that had descended upon the group after Ram Bahadur Gurung had shared the painful experience with them. He looked at each of them for assurance.

'You are absolutely right. That is the best way of coping with this unfortunate event.' Manohar BK extended his support.

'If you think that way, there is nothing to be worried about for us all, and I am really proud of you, my friend,' Sher Bikram Thapa said with an emotionally charged voice.

'I am really grateful that I have friends like you. You have always been there for me and it has been really helpful,' Ram Bahadur Gurung thanked his friends and genuine gratitude was clearly reflected in his eyes.

'We four are here for all four of us,' Krishna Sharma, Manohar BK and Sher Bikram Thapa said at the same time. Nothing more was needed to be said or done.

'It is getting late and I think we should make a move now,' Ram Bahadur Gurung said and got up from his seat. The others subsequently followed and they eventually walked out of the fast-food restaurant.

The train station was just around the corner. Manohar BK and Sher Bikram Thapa said their goodbyes and headed towards their respective destinations while Ram Bahadur Gurung and Krishna Sharma walked away as they lived nearby. It was already night by now and all the streets and nearby buildings had their lights on. The nightlife had just begun in Jordan, Yau Ma Tei, and Mong Kok areas.

It also happened to be the second time in a row that the four friends had missed the gathering on the rooftop. But amidst all the confusion, they did not even realize it.

Chapter 15

It was a Saturday afternoon one summer, the grocery store was not as busy as it normally was during the weekends, and only a few regular customers had frequented the store since morning. Not much had changed in the store for a very long time, and it had been selling similar items for years. The store catered mainly to the Nepalese community and hardly any locals sauntered in. The only noticeable change on that particular afternoon was the person tending the store. It was the patriarch, Krishna Sharma, who could always be seen at the store, but today it was Radha Sharma, his unmarried daughter, who was manning the store. Many had noticed Krishna Sharma's absence when they approached the counter to make their payments.

Radha had grown tired of answering the same question again and again. 'Where is the owner today?' people would ask and she would say, 'He is resting inside.'

The resting room was just behind the main store. It was not only poorly lit but also extremely hot and fitted with a set of sofas, a coffee table, and a TV rack on which a 32-inch old black and white TV had been placed. A portable side fan was on nearby, but it did not do much in terms of blowing air. The air-conditioning was turned on only when guests were visiting them in the private family area.

Krishna Sharma was still in a nightdress and wrapped in a Pashmina shawl. He was seated on a single sofa that was facing the store. Ram Bahadur Gurung was seated opposite him on another single sofa, and both Manohar BK and Sher Bikram Thapa were seated on the middle sofa. Krishna Sharma's friends had come to visit him at his home, and the guests had just been seated. They had brought for him a fruit basket as a courtesy.

Before anyone could say anything, Laxmi Sharma, the wife, appeared from the inner part of the house and politely asked if they cared for milk tea, water or anything else. Krishna Sharma told her, 'Get a glass of cold water first and then arrange the special ginger tea with some snacks,' she nodded and stepped away. Before too long, she reappeared again with a full tray and served them water. The room was getting cooler and more comfortable.

'What happened so suddenly?' Sher Bikram Thapa couldn't hold back his curiosity anymore and enthusiastically asked. Everyone turned towards him.

'You should have at least informed us before,' Ram Bahadur Gurung complained.

'Hope everything is okay by now,' Manohar BK added.

'I was faced with myriad problems, and they kept popping up one after another. I don't know how it all happened at the same time. It just won't stop,' Krishna Sharma replied in frustration.

'We heard that you were hospitalized for two days. What happened? Hope it was nothing serious and you are fine now,' Sher Bikram Thapa said in a concerned tone.

'Yes, it was a light stroke. While solving the barrage of problems, I did not take very good care of my health and ended up in the hospital. I rested for a few days and am fine now. There is nothing to be worried about,' Krishna Sharma explained.

'But how did this happen?' Ram Bahadur Gurung wanted to know.

'I have been running around, calling people and doing dozens of things all at once without resting. I was so busy and preoccupied that I didn't have time to go to the toilet and paid no attention at all to drinking and eating. I think I got dehydrated and collapsed on the chair. When I opened my eyes, I found myself in hospital and everyone was looking at me with worried faces.' Krishna Sharma took a deep breath and looked at his friends with weary eyes.

'What did the doctor say? Hope there were no other issues!' Manohar BK sympathized.

'Did you feel any pain afterwards?' Sher Bikram Thapa butted in.

'I didn't feel any particular pain but I was just tired. I could hardly move my fingers due to weakness. I was too fatigued and stressed, so I had a minor stroke, and needed rest, that's all. Thankfully, I got treated in time. Nothing to be worried about, all I need to do is to eat, drink and rest properly. And not stress too much,' Krishna Sharma said in a carefree manner, though his smile was forced.

'Even though you don't listen to us, you should at least listen to the doctor,' said Laxmi Sharma, who had just entered the room with a tray full of special tea, and had found enough courage to join the conversation. Had they been alone at home and it was not about his health, she would never have butted in. As she served them the special tea, everyone remained quiet and waited until she was done. In addition, she had also brought a big steel plate full of typical Nepalese snacks. 'Did I say anything wrong? Please tell me. Work is not everything. We should remain careful about our health. Especially at our age, we have to be extra cautious. Our men don't listen to us. I am sure that he will listen to you all, please make him understand, thank you,' she implored. All the men awkwardly smiled and nodded at her request.

'I know, I know, no need to repeat it.' Krishna Sharma pretended he was annoyed and ignored his wife. 'Please have tea,' he told his friends as he took his cup and started sipping from it. His wife stood there while the men drank tea.

'The tea is really nice, sister-in-law,' Ram Bahadur Gurung said.

'Today is our lucky day, thank you, sister-in-law!' Sher Bikram Thapa butted in.

'If we knew we could have such special tea here, we would have come almost every week, sister-in-law.' Manohar BK's words made Laxmi Sharma blush.

'You guys came here to meet my husband, drank the tea that I made, and I am really happy.' She thanked them and walked back to the kitchen with a beatific smile.

'It has already been a week and still we did not know anything about it,' Ram Bahadur Gurung lamented and the other two friends nodded in total agreement.

'I know, but it was not a big deal. Besides, I am recovering well and I think everything should be okay in the next few days. You guys are here anyway!' Krishna Sharma explained and tried to brush the matter off as if it were already a done deal.

'We are glad that all is fine now,' Manohar BK sighed with relief.

'What's more, my problems were of my own making and I had to deal with it in my own way,' Krishna Sharma said with a sense of guilt. He had realized he needed to be aware what he was doing more than anything else.

'We still don't know what exactly happened before the health incident. Hope it was not that serious and has been solved by now,' Sher Bikram Thapa dug in.

'You know my type of business, it is not as clear as it seems, and when something bad happens, we get hit hard. It was precisely what had happened to me, and it is just a matter of good and bad luck.' Krishna Sharma finally started to open up, and his friends paid great attention to what he had to say. He was, after all, the brightest of them all in business dealings and every story he narrated never ceased to amaze them.

'The problem started with our gold business.' Krishna Sharma hesitated for a while before starting again. 'It all started because of the unreliability of Nepal Airlines (NA). We all know how unreliable they are. The flight from Hong Kong had not only been delayed by an entire day, but it had also developed engine problems while in flight and had to be redirected to Dhaka in Bangladesh. By the time it finally reached Kathmandu, the customs officer we had made the deal with was no longer on duty and the next shift had begun. Needless to say, we couldn't make a new deal with him in time, hence the entire lot was confiscated. In addition, half of our foot soldiers, who were carrying our gold inside a camera of a particular make, fled and we failed to recover the gold from them as well. It was the beginning of the month, and we have been suffering ever since.'

'Have you managed to get the gold out of customs by now? Manohar BK inquired.

'We are still working on it. The continuous changes of the government back in Nepal also didn't help at all, and every time we were about to close the deal, something new happened, and it is still stuck in customs now,' Krishna Sharma explained.

'Hope the loss was not that big and you can clear it from customs soon. What kind of money are we are talking about here?' Ram Bahadur Gurung inquired.

'Something like a kilo or two in gold. But don't worry; not all of it is mine. It belongs to the syndicate and these people are influential enough to deal with the problem. It is just a matter of time. Sooner or later, we will get it,' Krishna Sharma said.

'You also said you had gold inside a camera, right? How did you do that?' Sher Bikram Thapa asked. He was curious.

'It's an old trick. We fixed a tael (37.80 grams) of gold inside the camera and asked people to carry it for us. We tell them it is just an ordinary camera and pay five hundred dollars each for the service. After all, each tourist must carry a camera, right?' Krishna Sharma explained with an impish look. Nepalese businessmen used ingenuity that couldn't be used elsewhere in business practices, and hit the jackpot.

'I didn't know gold was brought in that way,' Sher Bikram Thapa was taken aback.

'Remember when we were still in the army and going on long leave. One of my own relatives played the same trick on us. We didn't even know that we had actually become mules and were being used by him for a very long time,' Ram Bahadur Gurung said as he recalled his old days.

'I couldn't believe that the old rule is still in use now,' Manohar BK pitched in with a surprised look but he was not expecting a retort.

'If it works, why not try?' Krishna Sharma said and the ongoing conversation on the gold matter was concluded once and for all.

All that could be heard for a while were the slurping and chewing sounds the men made as they enjoyed the afternoon treat.

'Then what happened?' Ram Bahadur Gurung asked after gulping down a mouthful of that special tea with a soppy biscuit.

'The incumbent hakim of Nepal Airlines got transferred and the new one is playing a game of hard-to-get with us. And as you know, most of the stuff we sell here in the store comes from Nepal and without a helping hand from the Nepal Airlines chief, we will face problems,' Krishna Sharma replied.

'Since there is no other way except bringing goods in through Nepal Airlines, you must have a very good connection with them,' Manohar BK said, but did not elaborate further.

'And without a good relationship with the chief, you won't get a good deal and that can be bad for your business,' Ram Bahadur Gurung continued from where his friend had left off.

'We all know how our government officials work, the only way is the Nepalese way, and it means a deal under the table. Everybody is bent on milking the nation, I know this is not right, but we have no other choice. Do it or be left out,' Krishna Sharma lamented. Disappointment was clearly visible on his face.

'If that is the case, why not just go to his office and throw it in his face?' Sher Bikram Thapa suggested bluntly.

'Wish it were that easy. Despite all the rotten deeds inside, they pretend to be noble as a royal and preach rectitude like a priest. We Nepalese people have egos bigger than Mount Everest, everything can be forgotten and forgiven but ego mustn't be trampled upon, and that's why we have to tread very carefully.' Krishna Sharma was poetic.

'But you must have connections everywhere and it shouldn't be a problem for you,' Manohar BK suggested as they were fully aware of his ability as well as connections.

'I am working on it, my people are busy trying to figure out ways to get out of this situation and it should be okay very soon. It is just a matter of time before the chief came around. We just have to be patient,' Krishna Sharma said, trying to explain how things worked.

'He is new on the job and just being cautious,' Ram Bahadur Gurung pitched in.

'Exactly, everything will be just fine soon.' Krishna Sharma brushed it off as a trivial matter that could be easily handled by a seasoned veteran like him.

'Will you have a shortage on selling products?' Sher Bikram Thapa inquired.

'Not at all, it is not only for us but also for all the other Nepalese stores as well, and the loss is manageable,' Krishna Sharma said with confidence.

'Maybe you can buy products from our fellow countrymen from the New Territories,' Sher Bikram Thapa exhorted. 'I heard that our people are renting government lands in the New Territories for farming and supplying fresh vegetables and fruits. In fact, I already know some of them and, if necessary, I can help contact them.'

'Why not? I think that is a good idea. Please do.' Krishna Sharma's eyes lit up.

'I also heard that our people are farming and selling live chicken as well. They carry the chicken in baskets from the New Territories to the Jordan area here as well. Is that true?' Ram Bahadur Gurung asked, in an effort to spice up the conversation.

'I heard that as well. Just like back in the village in Nepal,' Manohar BK pitched in.

'Because of the Asian flu epidemic, selling live chickens is illegal in Hong Kong,' Krishna Sharma, the much-informed businessman, said.

'Try to say that to our people. It goes through one ear and

comes out through the other.' Ram Bahadur Gurung sounded rather sceptical but the reality was not that far away.

'Besides, I am a Brahmin. How can I do that so openly? I will be providing masala for unnecessary gossip and that is the last thing I need now,' Krishna Sharma elucidated his position on the newly suggested venture.

'No matter where we live, our social practices still influence us a great deal.' Manohar BK sighed. The effect of the feudal caste system was ubiquitous.

'I wonder how they get away with it in the Mass Transit Railways system in Hong Kong?' Sher Bikram Thapa asked.

'Maybe they use vehicles instead of MTR for transportation,' Manohar BK replied.

'Please have some more tea.' No one heard Laxmi Sharma come in with a huge teapot. She started pouring more tea into each cup. 'Shall I bring more snacks?' She asked once the teacups were duly filled, and everyone replied with a 'no'. They drank the tea in complete silence, and the conversation didn't resume until she had gone back to the kitchen.

'That was two weeks ago. By the way, how is sister-in-law doing? Hope she is coping well with the new situation at home,' Krishna Sharma said as he remembered, and everyone looked towards Ram Bahadur Gurung.

'She is just fine, thank you so much. We were sort of aware that this tragedy would happen sooner or later, and she was somehow prepared.' Ram Bahadur Gurung's explanation of his home situation provided some much-needed relief to his friends.

'That's good to know. Hope things are gradually getting sorted on your side as well,' Manohar BK said, looking at Sher Bikram Thapa.

'Thank you! I am almost recovered and still on official leave though and getting paid as well. The lawyer is already talking with the insurance people and, hopefully, it will be sorted out soon. The pain has not completely gone away though and it still hurts badly in the winter,' Sher Bikram Thapa replied and did some hand movements to show them it was fine.

'Was there any other problem or was that about it? You said it was two weeks ago. Hope the remaining two weeks went fine,' Ram Bahadur Gurung said.

'No, no, there was still more. It was like problems were lining up there, and in a hurry to trouble me,' Krishna Sharma continued with an ironic smile. 'The next was the hundi problem and it was a double whammy. Not only did our agent back in Kathmandu betray us and ran away with our money, but the banks in Hong Kong too suspended all our accounts and we could do nothing for the last two weeks. As you know, it is a very big operation and many people are involved, but we managed to capture the absconding guy within a week. The money was also recovered almost in full and we didn't suffer any loss. Similarly, the bank here in Hong Kong has promised to reopen our accounts by early next week. Therefore, we should be back in business soon. But to be honest with you, it scared the hell out of me and I am genuinely pleased and relieved that the ordeal is finally over.'

'The amount must have been quite big, ha…!' Manohar BK proclaimed.

'Almost five million HK dollars, but of course it belonged to the whole group, not just to me.' Krishna Sharma didn't hesitate in divulging his trade secret and his frankness surprised his friends. 'Still, it could have knocked us all out.'

'That's a lot of money. No wonder you got scared.' Sher Bikram Thapa sighed.

'Hundi must be a big business here, we can imagine. Since

our country has no proper facility of sending legal money through banks, hundi is the only way to send money back home, and when all of our people do that, it is obviously a lot,' Ram Bahadur Gurung conjectured. His logic was solid.

'And it is not only us, even the Indian, the Pakistani, the Bangladeshi and the Sri Lankan rely entirely on this system. So you have a general idea of how much money is flowing. It must be mind-boggling,' Manohar BK pitched in. He did some quick math that the others had already given up on before trying.

'But we are just small fish in a big ocean,' Krishna Sharma said, trying to clear his position.

'It must be connected with the gold market in India.' Sher Bikram Thapa had guessed it right. All the money collected here for hundi purposes are used to buy gold and is then sent back to India through many channels, including smuggling. It is where they make the big kill as India's gold market is huge. Nepal's market was like a few drops in the ocean.

'Sorry, but is it the main reason why local banks blacklisted us? Especially the big ones? They discriminate against us when we try to open a bank account. I am not sure but most people say so,' Ram Bahadur Gurung said with an innocent look on his face.

'It seems like it as we are definitely not on the terror list,' Manohar BK pitched in.

'We used to move hundreds of dollars in one transaction before and did at least a dozen or so in a day. Then they did change the system due to rampant money-laundering cases in Hong Kong, and new restrictions were applied. The most we could move was fifty thousand dollars in one transaction, but we still found ways to carry on our trade by using different account holders. After all, we South Asians are very good at finding loopholes and making the most of them by circumventing the rules. I can definitely say that hundi was the main reason why the banks are stricter now towards us.' Krishna Sharma's explanation put an end to the discussion and everyone agreed.

'Wish they didn't apply it as a wholesale practice and spared the innocent ones from this unnecessary ordeal. It is such a pity that they treat us all the same,' Ram Bahadur Gurung said with a grimace.

'They just need an excuse. It is always the minority groups that get whipped, and we are no different. Look how the locals, police, custom, immigration and other governmental officials treat us here,' Manohar BK said and it seemed as if he was venting his frustration at not being able to speak up in Hong Kong because he belonged to the minority community.

'Everybody looks down at us. Maybe that is the price of living in someone else's place,' Sher Bikram Thapa concluded with a sigh tinged with sadness and hopelessness. Had our country been rich and prosperous, nobody would have ventured out. Only migrants from poor nations could relate to this incessant pain.

'Shall I make more tea or bring anything else?' Laxmi Sharma was back in the room and dutifully asked the question like a good hostess. She wanted to make sure that her guests were happy and comfortable. 'Thank you so much, everything is enough, and you have been very kind!' Her guests spoke out in chorus, and she went back to the kitchen again with a smile.

'So many things happened all at the same time. No wonder you were seriously impacted. Many would have succumbed at the first hurdle. Not you. You had sufficient willpower, enough experience and the skill to handle such a tough situation. We are really happy and relieved that it is finally over. Hope things will get back to normal soon,' Ram Bahadur Gurung said, expressing his gratitude towards his friend's improving position. Needless to say, he was not only talking for himself but also on behalf of the other friends, and they all understood without having to utter a word.

'Yes, it was really hard,' Krishna Sharma sighed and continued, 'but it wasn't the end. There was still more and the last one was pretty scary too.'

'What? I thought the ones we already spoke about were more than enough. I can't believe there is more.' Sher Bikram Thapa was genuinely astounded.

'That's what we say in Nepali, '*Dasaa baaja bajaera audaina* (Bad luck doesn't come with a warning).' Manohar BK recited an old phrase that was in common parlance in Nepalese society.

'What happened? I just can't believe it,' Ram Bahadur Gurung said, his voice tinged with concern. All the signs of joy and happiness that they were experiencing hitherto suddenly evaporated and the room was filled with worried faces again.

'Don't worry. It is already over,' Krishna Sharma reassured them. His friends' concerned faces had not gone unnoticed by him. 'It was the refugee case, the asylum seekers in Hong Kong from South Asian nations. It wasn't me but one of my relatives who got involved in the case, and I got dragged into it just by the virtue of being related to him. They had brought in five people, two from Nepal, two from India and one from Bangladesh, who got caught by Immigration. They were held at the Hong Kong airport for two days and when they were about to be put on a return flight back home, they claimed asylum and new cases were registered accordingly. The deportation was somehow stopped, but one of them was caught off guard during the interrogation, and he took my name by mistake. As a result, the officers got suspicious, took it as a case of human trafficking, and I was summoned by the police.'

'How is that possible? Since you had no involvement, it is impossible for them to know your name,' Manohar BK butted in.

'My surname, of course! After all, we have so many people in our country with the same surname. What's more, thanks to the plethora of our Gods and Goddesses, we all have the same first name as well. How many Krishna, Ram, Bishnu, Hari, Gopal and so on do we have in our society? Even one village might have half a dozen or so. Not surprising at all,' Krishna Sharma said with a shrug and threw both hands up to prove his point.

'You are absolutely right! Not surprising at all. You just say a name and bingo. All that the police had to do was to run a search of their record and round them all up at one go. We should have just a few with similar names and checking on them is not a problem at all,' Ram Bahadur Gurung said.

'How many Krishna Sharmas do we have in Hong Kong? One or two maximum! No wonder they found you so easily,' Sher Bikram Thapa said.

'They kept me in a small room the entire afternoon, asked thousands of questions that I had no answers for, and even used scaremongering tactics to such an extent that few times I was genuinely scared. They even threatened me with a jail term and tried to make me confess. They didn't even let me eat, drink or see other people, and I had to stay in that small room the entire afternoon and night. But of course, since I was innocent, I didn't buckle under pressure. In the end, when they got nothing out of me and were convinced of my innocence, they let me go home without slapping any charges on me. I was allowed to return home early the next day. I was so drained physically and emotionally from the ordeal that my body simply gave up, and I fainted right here on the floor. And found myself on a hospital bed and, as the saying goes, the rest is history. But I am fine now, there is nothing to be worried about, and I will be as strong and fit as I was before in just a few days,' Krishna Sharma explained in a single breath. However, the stress of repeating the unfortunate event was taking a toll on him and his pale face was testimony to that.

'But that was wrong. As the saying goes, until proven guilty, everyone is innocent, and they cannot treat us like criminals,' Manohar BK complained.

'Exactly! I think you should make an official complaint,' Sher Bikram Thapa added.

'That is a non-starter. They can keep you there for the next twenty-four hours in case of suspicion alone and the interrogation process was according to the rule of law. Unless you were tortured and bodily harmed, there is not much of a case against them,' Ram Bahadur Gurung explained. Clearly, he had some idea about the processes. But those were things that could easily be learned by watching news and TV serials on a regular basis.

'He is absolutely right. They were very strict at the beginning but loosened up subsequently as they realized that I wasn't lying. They provided food and drink towards the end and expressed their gratitude and thanked me for my help and assistance with the investigation. They even apologized and I have decided to forget about it, just like a bad dream and nothing more. Sometimes I think we have to let things go, and it can save us from many unnecessary troubles in life. And that was a life lesson that I will remember for life, and I suggest you guys take this advice as well.' Krishna Sharma seemed not only grateful but proved to be a good example of how life can be a teacher in many ways. Defeat doesn't always yield loss. Sometimes even ordeals can become a blessing in disguise and the reward is unbelievable.

'Did you know the person who had brought them in there as asylum seekers?' Sher Bikram Thapa inquired.

'How much were they charging for the service?' Manohar BK asked before his friend could answer the first question and everyone waited attentively for his answer.

'Of course, I know him. He was one of my distant relatives, and in fact he did learn the business from me.' Krishna Sharma tried to brush off the question. He was finding it quite hard to handle. Not because he wanted to hide things from his friends, but the culprit was none other than his own son-in-law, and he had difficulty naming him. He had no intention of badmouthing the young man, at least for the sake of his own daughter, and decided to remain quiet for good. 'The current rate is said to be around four to five lakh Nepali rupees for each head, which is approximately thirty-five thousand HK dollars, and whether the new arrivals did succeed or not in entering Hong Kong, the agent got to keep the money regardless. The agent has no risk and it is the clients who are risking everything. Yet, people still line up behind the agents in great numbers.'

'It all comes back to the situation of a nation itself again, isn't it? Nepal must be one of those unfortunate nations in this world where human traffickers are worshipped as saviours. When destiny betrays you even before you were born, what can you expect with life other than destitution, hopelessness and indignity? Had our nation been good, we wouldn't have been forced to come here and live a life of a third-class citizen, right?' Ram Bahadur Gurung said, and it was obvious by his tone that the topic had made him philosophical.

'If you usurp someone else's place, injustice and unfair treatment are the norm of life. But the problem lies somewhere else. Our perspective of planning is very short-sighted, and we only see things that are in front of our eyes. We never look far enough, we never see things in the long term, and it is this myopic view that holds us back. The other problems are our fakeness and pretence. No matter what low and odd jobs we do here abroad, we show up as we had just returned home from a goldmine, and make it sound very glamorous. As a result, it creates a false impression that life abroad must be really good, a paradise. Money must be growing on trees, and everybody wants to benefit from it. Nobody has the guts to tell the truth, pretences create illusions, and that very illusion has unfortunately become an aspiration for the whole nation. It is where the real harm is done, our youths are wasted in foreign countries, and the nation is somehow stuck at the far end without a future.' It seemed like Manohar BK had also become philosophical, and he simply had to let it out.

Just then, Sher Bikram Thapa chimed in as how could he have been left behind? 'Showing off runs in our blood. We will die but we won't stop showing off. And like you have already said, it is this bad habit that is harming us more than anything else. We make everyone jealous back in Nepal, no wonder they hate us so much. We work as security guards, construction workers, and cleaners here, and when we go back to Nepal, we act like we're royalty. We compete with our neighbours on such frivolous things like whose house is bigger, who wears more gold jewellery, whose car is nicer, who has more plots of land in the city, and so on. We are always busy outsmarting each other while forgetting everything else in life.'

'Something very bizarre someone was said to have done was this: he flew back to his village in a helicopter and threw money from above. How stupid is that? I just couldn't believe it. For God's sake, why would you do something like that?' Krishna Sharma said with disgust on his face.

'That is actually true. That person is from near our village,' Ram Bahadur Gurung said. He was feeling awkward and bad at the same time.

'Just unbelievable!' Sher Bikram Thapa agreed.

'There must be plenty of such stories involving our people upon their return to Nepal. I think we can easily spend days by just talking about such antics,' Manohar BK said with an ironic smile and signalled they were getting to the end of this unwanted discussion. 'We, Nepalese people, have more such unfortunate incidents than real achievements in life, and that truth alone is one of the greatest ironies of our not-so-great lives. Hate it or not, truth is always the truth and it cannot be hidden for too long.

'By the way, what happened to those fake asylum seekers

then? And how did they manage to get your name in the first place?' Sher Bikram Thapa wanted to know. The conversation got steered back to the issue at hand.

'They were locked up for a few more days while the police and immigration officers continued their investigation and were eventually put under the UNHCR until the case was verified. As such cases take years before the final verdict is out, the lives of those involved are stuck forever in limbo. They can neither return home nor work here. Living as a normal citizen is a far-fetched dream. Sadly, nobody knows this fact back in Nepal and everybody ends up with a life that has no future,' Krishna Sharma said. Suddenly he sounded emotional and did not sound like the man who had mostly benefitted from other peoples' weaknesses.

'Some of the asylum seekers have been here for decades, and their future is still riddled with uncertainty,' Ram Bahadur Gurung pitched in. The Nepalese community in Jordan area was notoriously known for illegally hiring asylum seekers.

'They are not only cheap to hire but also easy to exploit,' Manohar BK added.

'Oh, sorry...! I almost forgot to reply to that.' Krishna Sharma apologized on his temporary lack of concentration and eventually replied, 'As this job of recruiting overseas job seekers is discreetly done, it is mostly the familiar ones that got involved, and one of them happened to be our distant relative. He, of course, knew me very well and when he got caught at the airport, he panicked and thought that maybe taking my name would help him. It was a mistake on his part and when he realized it, he instantly withdrew his statement, hence, I was spared the ordeal.'

'Thank God, the misunderstanding got sorted in time.' Sher Bikram Thapa was genuinely relieved.

'It is always our own people who take advantage of our naivety and lack of knowledge about overseas jobs. We marvel at our own peoples' misery and ruin many lives. Whenever there is a tragedy, whether it is in the Gulf nations, Malaysia, Hong Kong, Japan or South Korea, the culprit behind the incident is always our own people, and it disgusts me. But what can I do? We haven't even sorted our own lives, what chances are there for us?' Ram Bahadur Gurung lamented his own position. But he was not only talking about himself. Most of the Nepalese community in Hong Kong was more or less in a similar situation.

'Our people are good to the whole world but to ourselves. We are the nation of xenophiles and we take pride on being nicer to all. But when it comes to our own people, we take a 360-degree turn, and become complete jerks,' Manohar BK said.

'Another reason is we only cheat our own people, the others are too smart for their own good,' Sher Bikram Thapa threw in with a sarcastic laugh. The others agreed.

'Remember the popular saying in our community. We have two types of teeth like an elephant: one for showing only, the other for chewing. Almost every Nepalese has a second business on the side, a rather secret one and that is where they make the biggest kill.' Krishna Sharma put the kibosh on the conversation by this saying. The greatest thing about us Nepalese people is the tendency of being able to laugh at our own, and we usually do it to such an extent that most of the time we don't even realize it.

'Do you have to report back to the hospital again? Are you still taking your medicines?' Ram Bahadur Gurung asked as he wanted to change the subject. As the discussion was about to come to an end, his timing was perfect. Everyone waited for Krishna Sharma to answer.

'No, no, all is fine. I just need to take some vitamin pills and nothing else,' Krishna Sharma replied casually. They remained there for at least half an hour more and talked about other trivial issues. By the time they did finally say goodbye and headed home, it was almost 7 p.m. But what they didn't realize was that it was for the third time in a row they had missed the usual gathering at the rooftop, and three months had already passed since their last visit.

Chapter 16

It had been a week since the major typhoon had struck Hong Kong and most of the damage and debris caused by the typhoon had been cleared. The aftermath of a typhoon is like a war zone as streets are littered with fallen objects and garbage, and fallen trees that obstruct the road have to be removed for better traffic movement. Despite a direct hit, which was rare, Hong Kong was spared from major disaster with just a few damaged buildings here and there. The city heaved a huge sigh of relief and carried on with life as usual.

It was around 2 p.m., the streets were busy on a typical Saturday afternoon with shoppers and pedestrians scampering about, and the weather was as hot and humid as it had always been. The family had some guests that afternoon, and Manohar BK was tending to them in the living room while Parbati BK worked in the kitchen. Both children, Michael and Donna BK, were outside. The guests were seated on the sofa by the window. The wooden coffee table near the sofa had a fruit basket on it. Manohar BK was seated on the sofa next to the coffee table, facing his guests.

Krishna Sharma started the conversation, as usual, 'The typhoon was quite scary, ha...! Thank God it wasn't as bad as it had been initially anticipated. I think we were lucky to be spared with not much major loss and damage.'

'We rarely get a direct hit, and this time we were quite lucky we didn't get thrashed as predicted. It was a close shave though,' Ram Bahadur Gurung agreed.

'Thankfully, it was night-time when it passed through Hong Kong and many were inside their homes, so there was less damage,' Sher Bikram Thapa added.

'Hong Kong was genuinely fortunate this time. We could see down the streets from up here. During typhoons the streets are empty and fully deserted. The wind howled the entire night.' Manohar BK said with a scared look.

'Glad that it is over now and we all can go back to our daily life as usual,' Krishna Sharma said.

'How is your health? Hope you are fully recovered by now,' Manohar BK asked Krishna Sharma with a curious look. He was genuinely concerned about his friend's well-being.

'It is not a big deal, I am just fine, and there is nothing to be worried about.' He brushed off the health issue as if it were nothing more than a temporary cough that comes with old age, and nobody should be concerned about it.

'Glad to hear that,' Manohar BK said with a sigh of relief and turned towards other friends who had health problems. 'Hope your hand is okay now. What about the legal issue? Hope it is going well as planned.'

'Oh, no worries, my hand is fine. It is only in the winter that it hurts and I suppose it is for life,' Sher Bikram Thapa replied without any difficulty. He had become accustomed to the situation he was in and talking about the problem was a lot easier than before.

'It seemed like a run of bad luck for us friends. It started with Sher first, and then, me and Krishna, and now it's your turn.' Ram Bahadur Gurung had suddenly become serious and expressed the fear that had been plaguing him for a long time.

'It had been in my mind for quite a while, but I didn't dare to say it as I was afraid of having more bad luck,' Sher Bikram Thapa found the courage to say.

'On the bright side, it at least shows how we are fully connected,' Krishna Sharma joked and it made everyone laugh for the moment.

'I could not have believed that but when it actually did happen to us, I had to believe in it and the bad luck simply didn't end until it hit all four of us. It was like a chain reaction, one after another, and made a complete round as if it had been planned by some sort of divine power. You won't believe it until it actually happens to you and our position is no different.' Manohar BK sounded surprised and relieved as he talked, and genuinely pleased that he could get it off his chest once and for all.

'What really happened? Hope the loss was manageable,' Ram Bahadur Gurung had finally asked the main question, which was why they had come to meet their friend in trouble. Unfortunately, it had become a kind of routine, and it was already the third visit they had taken within a few months' period. It was their last visit.

Before Manohar BK could reply, Parvati BK came in with a tray full of cups and snacks and placed it on the coffee table before she served them one cup each. It was hot milk coffee with typical Nepalese snacks, and it was only here at Manohar and Parvati BK's place where they were served with such high-quality coffee.

'Thank you so much, sister-in-law, for such nice coffee. It is only here from your hand we can have the opportunity, and we will savour it for a very long time,' Krishna Sharma said in a complimentary tone as he took the first sip and appreciated it as if it were the best thing in the world. Only he could get away with such a cheap act.

'Thank you so much, sister-in-law.' Ram Bahadur Gurung and Sher Bikram Thapa repeated the gratitude politely. Regardless of age or relationship, they would call all wives 'sister-in-law' with affection, and the title fitted nicely for all occasions. Given that it was a men's gathering, she greeted them with grace and left them undisturbed as she returned to the kitchen with a smile.

'It was quite an unexpected and unbelievable incident. We simply didn't see it coming and almost got pummelled by it,' Manohar BK finally opened up. His words had truth and pain to such an extent that everyone's attention was fully centred on him. 'It was a Saturday night and the eatery was full of diners, and everyone was really busy. Then, to the utter surprise of us all, a group of diners suddenly freaked out in such a way that it disturbed all the diners and created a scene. They found not only one, two but three objects in the meal – a dead cockroach in the mutton curry, a metal screw in a samosa, and a syringe inside the naan, all on the same table.

I was gob-smacked and didn't know how to react. But the next hour or so was probably one of the worst periods of my entire restaurateur career. It was chaos. Everybody was upset, stopped eating, and started making threatening remarks. I pleaded for patience, tried to explain the mistake and genuinely apologized. But nobody was ready to listen. In desperation, I even offered free meals as the last resort but still nobody took heed. At the end, police were called in, the duty officers from the health and hygiene department had arrived, and everyone was cleared out. At the same time, I was taken to the police station for further inquiry, the restaurant was sealed off until further notice, and my whole world came crashing down even before I could fully realize it.'

'And you didn't even bother to inform us while it was all happening?' Krishna Sharma jumped in with thunder and everyone followed him.

'It was like a bad dream, you could see what was happening but had no control in preventing it, and the only thing I could think of was my restaurant and nothing else. And how could I remember calling you all in such a condition?' he almost cried.

'Besides, we could have done nothing to prevent it from happening anyway,' Ram Bahadur Gurung pitched in and they couldn't agree more.

'When did you return home from the police station then? Hope it wasn't for too long,' Sher Bikram Thapa inquired.

'By the time they did finally let me go, it was six in the morning, after spending the entire night at the police station,' Manohar BK replied in a tired tone.

'What did they want to know from you? Obviously, it wasn't your fault,' Krishna Sharma asked with curiosity.

'They asked so many questions during the investigation that I hardly remembered anything else. They were pretty aggressive as well as intimidating in the beginning and wanted to know why and how such objects got into the kitchen. Was it an act of carelessness or was it intentional? Who worked in the kitchen? What system did we apply? Who supervised the kitchen? Whose duty was it to check on food and other stuff in the kitchen? Why were there such incidents? Did you plan for it? Were there drugs? Were there any drug peddlers? Was my employee a junkie? Did I handle drugs? Why was there a syringe? Did I know or harbour any drug dealers? And the questioning continued until they were fully convinced that I was innocent, and had nothing that could be used against me. In the end, they let me go and told me that they would call me again, if necessary,' Manohar BK said in an agitated tone. He was still disturbed about the unprecedented ordeal.

'Then what happened?' Sher Bikram Thapa asked with concern.

'Then, I went to the restaurant on my way back home. When

I saw the restaurant's main entrance fully sealed off with a notice, I finally realized that something terrible had happened to me, and I needed to find out why. Someone was playing a very nasty game behind my back; those objects didn't get into the food on their own; someone had to have done it. Who could that be? I had to find that out before my restaurant was forced to close down once and for all. And for the last four weeks, it was all I did and I am glad that it is almost done now,' Manohar BK said with a huge sigh of relief.

'It is pretty obvious that someone had planted them,' Ram Bahadur Gurung concluded.

'It must be the finding of the syringe that attracted the police's interest,' Krishna Sharma added before Manohar BK could reply.

'Exactly, coincidence can happen once but not thrice. That is obvious,' Sher Bikram Thapa said with a confidence that he had not shown in years.

'Yes, it was sabotage. A well-planned one indeed and it almost brought me to heel,' Manohar BK said triumphantly.

'But who could be your enemy? I don't see any other Nepalese restaurants around here?' Krishna Sharma was genuinely baffled by the progress of the story.

'It was a long story. I had the same dilemma in the beginning and no matter how hard I tried, I couldn't find any logic that would explain my situation. Besides, I didn't know many people around here in Wan Chai. I have offended no one, and I was probably the nicest guy around here in this industry. Who could it be? Who wants to harm me? And why does he want to sabotage my restaurant? I had many questions but no answers. I spent many restless nights and days searching for the right answer. But nothing changed until that call from the police and everything has started to make sense ever since.' Manohar BK stopped for a moment and took a big gulp of the coffee from his cup.

'Did the police catch anyone?' Sher Bikram Thapa jumped in.

'Yes, and it was none other than my own chief cook,' Manohar BK said, a look of dismay on his face.

'Wait, as far as I can remember, it was the Nepalese guy, right?' Krishna Sharma wondered. 'But why would he do that?'

'Yes, I was flabbergasted when I heard it for the first time,' Manohar BK said.

'He must have some reason to have committed such a heinous crime against his own boss,' Ram Bahadur Gurung pitched in.

'He is the same person that you brought from Nepal, gave him a chance in life and he did this to you! It's like biting the hand that feeds you,' Sher Bikram Thapa said with a solemn look and took a mouthful of coffee to calm himself down.

'I think it was a little of everything. Greed, gullibility, circumstance as well as short-sightedness that played a part,' Manohar BK tried to be philosophical.

'How did they find out? It certainly wasn't that easy,' Krishna Sharma inquired.

'It took a week before the police got their big break. Once they got on the right track, the dots started connecting on their own and the whole drama unfolded in front of them like a big picture on a screen,' Manohar BK said. 'He was just a pawn in a big plan masterminded by the owner of the restaurant next door. It was a local Chinese restaurant serving fresh seafood and doing pretty well for years. Then the owner saw my restaurant doing well as well and couldn't stand it for too long. After all, I was an outsider who was trampling upon his turf. He felt threatened and insecure. Therefore, he hatched a plan, sent his cook out to befriend my cook, and used him when the right opportunity struck. They lured him with money, instructed the poor guy when, how and what to do, all in detail, and sent their lackeys to my restaurant as customers. It was in fact quite a meticulous and well-executed plan. Had it not been the cook himself, who did eventually crack under intense police interrogation, they might have succeeded in their plan. But luck was with me and truth always prevails. The cook couldn't take the pressure, spilled the beans and begged for mercy.'

'That's great. Hope all the bad people were arrested and made to pay for their crime,' Ram Bahadur Gurung said with a sigh of relief. The others echoed the same sentiment.

'Yes, everyone involved was taken away by the police for further inquiry and final charges were slapped accordingly. But it might take a while before the whole case is resolved and everyone involved is punished,' Manohar BK explained.

'How much was the cook paid to do the job?' Sher Bikram Thapa asked.

'Twenty-thousand HK dollars!' Manohar BK replied.

'That is not much. What is wrong with him?' Krishna Sharma butted in.

'He is at home now without work. I am working with the police now so they can drop all the charges against him and have him come back to work once the restaurant is reopened again. As he was new here and used by others, the possibility of proving his innocence was quite high, and if the worst comes to worst, he might have to pay some penalty.' Manohar BK said this so casually that the others were surprised.

'Why are you helping him after what he did to you?' Everyone asked the same question at the same time. His words puzzled them.

'Relax. I know why you were reacting that way. Please let me explain,' Manohar BK said. 'He did it out of desperation. He is not a bad man; he is a very simple man indeed. Circumstances had forced his hand to do such stupid things. All in all, it was his naivety and nothing else. We all know what our community is like here in Hong Kong. Most of the real Gurkhas have already moved to the UK after they won the right of abode, and the ones who remained here are mostly the newly arrived ones. They are also known as the fake ones, mostly with purchased birth certificates, sham marriages and made-up children. The ongoing rate of fake spouses is said to be around fifteen to twenty lakhs, which is approximately 105–143k HK dollars, and said to be a common practice among our people. His brother-in-law, his wife's younger brother, happened to be associated with such a sham marriage, and the agent was asking for a big sum before further commitment. As you know, the spouses have to go to Immigration for visa renewal, and the sponsors are refusing to do so until their demand of a big pay is met. This has become a new way of extorting more money from the fake spouses within our community in Hong Kong. His brother-in-law was the victim of such fraud and he just buckled under the pressure.'

'That is quite understandable but still…!' Krishna Sharma left the sentence unfinished.

'He came to my place, profusely apologized and cried in shame,' Manohar BK explained. 'He also begged for another chance, and I sincerely do believe that he will prove me right in the future.'

'You are absolutely right to make such a decision. I think he will appreciate the job more in the future and remain grateful for life.' Sher Bikram Thapa endorsed his friend; he had no reason to have doubts on his decision.

'That is the right decision. I have heard many such stories involving our community members. It is so disgusting, but some are said to be in such agreement where even actual siblings appear as husband and wife in front of Immigration and nobody knows for sure what is real and what is not. Gurung became Thapa, Rai became Magar, Limbu became Pun, and so on. I personally think it is not only wrong but also shameful to behave that way. I don't understand why our people stoop so low for money. But of course, who am I to complain? Nobody listens to anybody like us. All I wanted to say was this – We are not back in Nepal anymore; we are in Hong Kong and we should start behaving like those in Hong Kong. That's all,' Ram Bahadur Gurung signed off thus, but everyone present was clueless about how to apply that in real life.

Parvati BK walked in with a thermos full of freshly made coffee, filled up each cup and went back to the kitchen again without uttering a word. The aroma of freshly brewed coffee was soothing to the senses.

'Selling Hong Kong ID cards is a business for some, big houses are built in Kathmandu from this trade alone, and many people have become rich,' Krishna Sharma said in agreement.

'We have changed homes, places and even our lives, but our typical Nepalese mentality remained unchanged. We are stuck there forever,' Manohar BK summarized.

'That's why our society never progresses,' Sher Bikram Thapa pitched in.

The next few moments passed away without any talk; everyone was busy enjoying the fresh cup of coffee.

'So, what is the status of the case now? Hope it can be settled soon,' Krishna Sharma said with concern.

'I told the police that I don't want any trouble. I don't believe in revenge, I don't want enmity with anyone, and I just want to move on with my life. If my decision of closing down the case would benefit all and bring peace among us, I am ready to take that very decision and forget everything about the whole incident. All I want is to get my restaurant back and start working again. The police insisted on pressing charges but when I made my position clear to them again, they finally relented and all the cases were eventually dropped. The Chinese restaurant owner came to apologize, all his men were released as well, and we have actually become good neighbours. As a result, everything is fine now and the case is almost closed. I am also glad and relieved that the ordeal is finally over and I am going to start working again,' Manohar BK briefly explained. His face sparkled as a huge weight had lifted off his shoulders.

'That is quite interesting. You let them all off the hook without any fine or punishment? Forgiveness is great but people take it differently. Hope some don't take your kindness as weakness,' Sher Bikram Thapa said, clearly worried about Manohar's decision and whether it was a good or bad one.

'It is called guilt of the conscience. Even if we don't express it doesn't mean we don't have it. And I think it will certainly work in the long term. Because we cannot run away from our own consciences for a very long time and, sooner or later, our inner conscience will catch up with us for all the decisions of our lives, whether right or wrong,' Ram Bahadur Gurung tried to explain the reason behind Manohar BK's decision and everyone agreed.

'Thanks for clearing that up. The police also had similar comments. After all we also have to respect our laws, and they were talking about arranging a sort of fine that could be used as a way out for all parties. What's more, it could also be used as a settlement for the loss that accrued due to the sudden closure of the restaurant. I am not sure what amount that would be, the police will inform me when it is decided. But I am fine with whatever decision they might take and I am readying myself to move on again,' Manohar BK said with contentment on his face.

'Yes, I think you should be compensated for your losses if not more. The police are definitely right on that part for sure. Whether it is reward or punishment, men should take responsibility for their actions,' Krishna Sharma said with a smile.

'When is the restaurant opening again? Since you were not the one to have committed the crime, there shouldn't be a problem on reopening it again, right?' Sher Bikram Thapa asked.

'It should be soon, I suppose. The health and hygiene department said so. They are still waiting for clearance from the police and it should be arriving soon. Just a matter of a few days at the most.' Manohar BK sounded hopeful.

'That is certainly good news. Hope the losses were manageable,' Ram Bahadur Gurung said.

'After observing the past events, I have learned to see things from a very different perspective and that has made a big difference in my life. Instead of counting the losses and making ourselves miserable, I said to myself that it could have been a lot worse. I am glad it was finally over. Sometimes, we actually win even after a big loss and not all the wins can be measured with money. It is the experience, opportunity and life-lesson that it provides us that are priceless. I think it is what I gained and I am happy with that,' Manohar BK said. Hearing him talk in such a positive tone his friends were genuinely happy for him.

'Very nicely said and true as well. Being able to see things from a different and positive way in such an adversity is already a very big thing, and you should be applauded just for that. We are really happy for you,' Ram Bahadur Gurung said and everyone nodded in agreement.

'I hope it signals the end of our bad luck. It started with me and ended with you after paying an unwelcome visit to all four of us. Let's bid goodbye to our uninvited guest once and for all and hope that our paths never cross again in the future,' Sher Bikram Thapa said in jest, but nothing could have reflected their situation better than what he had just presented, and everyone wished for that to become a reality at the earliest.

'It was a testing time for us all. We have endured great losses as well as pain. But in the end, it made us not only stronger but also wiser and that can be a great asset dealing with similar situations in the future. Most importantly, it brought us even closer, and our friendship has become way stronger than it was before. Our presence here is already proof of that special bond, and it can only grow stronger henceforth. Just like what he had said a few moments before, we have gained a lot in this aspect and we should be grateful for that. For our long-term friendship, let's make a toast, and drink to it as a promise as well as a wish for it to last a lifetime. Cheers!' Krishna Sharma raised his cup with an emotionally charged speech and they duly obliged.

'Cheers!' The whole place echoed and subsequently filled with soft laughter and light banter that had been missing for some time. They conversed for some more time and eventually returned home by 7 p.m. It was certainly a nice gathering and they hardly had time for other things. What they didn't remember was that this was the fourth time in a row they had missed the special gathering at the rooftop place, and they had no idea that they were about to miss it once and for all.

Chapter 17

The building caught fire in the dark of night, and burned down the whole rooftop. Yet, except for the people from the nearby buildings, nobody came to know. When morning dawned, the only thing that remained was the pile of ashes from the burning. Thankfully, the fire didn't spread to other parts of the building; only the illegal storage structure on the rooftop was completely demolished. Since it was an illegal structure, nobody, including the owner who had built it, came forward and the possibility of keeping a record on it was lost even before it could be started. As a result, officials were not able to answer such important questions, such as who the owner was, what was stored there, whether anyone was living there during the fire, and what the loss was, etc., etc. Most importantly, the fire department had no answers for such questions: how did the fire start? Was anyone injured? Was there any foul play? Or, was it just an accident? It required a thorough investigation to get the answers.

All of Hong Kong was awakened by this bad news, the aftermath of the fire was repeatedly displayed on TV screens throughout the day, and people could hardly miss the building. Krishna Sharma noticed the fire scenes at the familiar building as he opened the grocery store for business and instantly realized that the fire had destroyed their favourite haunt. As his eyes were glued to the TV screen, he couldn't believe what he was seeing: the special place where they had been gathering for so long had turned into a pile of ashes. The news was shocking and left him unable to react for a while.

He didn't know how long he had been standing in front of the TV screen. It was only when a customer asked for his payment receipt that he stopped and slowly walked back to the counter. It was obvious from the way he was watching the TV screen that something terrible had befallen him. Once the customer had left the store, he picked up the phone and tried to call his other friends. As both Ram Bahadur Gurung and Sher Bikram Thapa had returned from night duty and were asleep, he could only find Manohar BK at that hour and they expressed regret in losing their favourite meeting place on the rooftop. After they spoke, they informed the other two friends via text.

There was no time for further mourning. Life without the special meeting place at the rooftop had already become a reality, and they had to accept the fact like grown-ups and move on. Yet a nagging sense of loss lingered for the rest of the day, and they could hardly concentrate on other things. It was almost 3 p.m. when the other two friends responded. They were equally shocked and saddened by the unprecedented loss and didn't know how it could be recovered anytime soon.

The Namaste Club, the anvil that had helped forge their friendship so far, had been destroyed. They had never been delivered such a rude shock before.

Chapter 18

It was a rare Sunday afternoon when Ram Bahadur Gurung was not on duty and was at home with his family. Not to waste the opportunity, Gauri Maya Gurung had arranged for a family gathering and both their son and daughter-in-law had arrived as well. It had been a long time since they had such a gathering, and special dishes had been prepared for the occasion. Mother, son and daughter-in-law were busy in the kitchen, but not all were cooking. Mother was doing all the cooking, her Chinese daughter-in-law was looking and learning from the mother-in-law, and the son had to remain close by to act as an interpreter. The mother wasn't good at Chinese and English, the daughter-in-law didn't understand Nepali well, so they had to take the son's help. It was quite an interesting scene, both sides had to wait until the middleman could explain, and the conversation took much longer than usual. Yet, nobody was complaining.

While they cooked in the kitchen, Ram Bahadur Gurung made himself comfortable on the sofa and watched TV. It had been sometime before he had the opportunity of being able to put his legs up and he was certainly relishing the moment. Most importantly, all members of his family were at home and he couldn't ask for more.

'Here is your afternoon tea, Dad, please enjoy!' Trimol Gurung, the son, said with a broad smile and handed his father the tea mug.

'Thank you!' Ram Bahadur Gurung grabbed the handle and took a cautious sip from the mug. 'Do you remember this mug?' he asked, remembering something.

'Not exactly!' the son said as obliviously as he could. 'What's special about the mug?' he asked with a curious look.

'That is your father's favourite mug, and he always drinks from it.' It was the mother who shouted from the kitchen, despite how close she was.

'Oh, I didn't know that,' the son casually said and turned around.

'Someone very special gave it to me as a birthday present,' Ram said enthusiastically and his memories brightened up his face.

'You must have loved that person very much then.' The daughter-in-law commented from the kitchen.

'More than anything else in this world,' the old man said affectionately, and felt the mug with both hands as if he were actually feeling that special person.

It was a simple round-shaped white clay mug with a handle and had a sketch of an old man and two young boys in black.

Gauri Maya came out of the kitchen and began to tell a story. 'We were still in the Shek Kong army camp, it was a Sunday, and we all, including Anmol, but without your father, went to the Yuen Long market as we used to do when we had a holiday. There was a big old shopping mall where we could buy almost everything from clothes, shoes, bed sheets, children's clothes and toys, vegetables and fruits, and other household products. All the Gurkha soldiers from the army camp used to buy stuff there before returning to Nepal. We were visiting one of those department stores where we saw that mug and you, Trimol, insisted on buying it before we could go anywhere. Since we were not going anywhere before getting the cup, we eventually bought it since it was right there on the counter, and you gave it to your father as a birthday present. I didn't know where you got that idea. It wasn't even his birthday and only children used to have birthday celebrations in those days, not the parents. And as the saying goes, the rest is history and your father has been taking care of it as if it is the most precious thing in his life. Now you know why it is so special for him!'

The story moved everyone emotionally, especially after Trimol translated it for his wife.

'Sorry, I had no intention whatsoever of hurting your feelings,' Trimol said as he sat down next to his father. 'It just slipped from my mind and I hope you don't mind.' The son sat next to his father and held his hand.

'There is nothing to be sorry about, son. After all, it has already been so long anyway! Please don't worry!' the father said with teary eyes, pressed his son's hand and affectionately kept on looking at him.

'This story is about the three of us, you, me and your brother Anmol. I remember it now. Wherever Anmol is now, I sincerely wish him well and hope for the best,' Trimol said softly as he pointed to the mug.

'Yes, wherever he might be, I wish him well and God bless him,' the father repeated. The memory of his deceased son was the hardest to bear, and it made everyone cry.

The place was suddenly filled with an aura of sadness, and needed a quick fix before it ruined the whole atmosphere. It was supposed to be a happy family gathering after all, and sadness had no place in the Gurung household.

'Let bygones be bygones and let's not ruin our day by talking about sad things from our past. We have finally got a chance at some happiness. How is work going for you and Teresa? What are your plans for the future? And when is the big day coming?' Ram had changed the topic right away, and did his best to appear as jovial as an old man possibly could.

'What big day are you talking about?' the son asked with an uneasy look and squirmed in his seat. He somehow knew his father was talking about children. The sudden aberration also caught both ladies, who had gone back to the kitchen, off-guard, especially the daughter-in-law. Despite the language barrier, Teresa was the most affected one and it was clearly seen on her blushing face. She knew what her father-in-law was referring to.

'You have already been married for some time now, you should start planning for the future and this thing shouldn't take too long. Trust me, we don't get any younger anymore and the older you get the harder it will be,' Ram explained but he refrained from being specific intentionally.

'Please, Dad, don't worry about it. Like you said, it is not the right time for discussing it and trust me, we will have our plans worked out soon.' Despite being from a totally different generation than his parents, the son did in fact understand his parent's concern and tried to make them understand his position.

'Is it your wife who is not ready yet? If so, just tell me, I will have a talk with her, and I am pretty sure that she will listen and try her best to fulfil this old man's wish,' his father said with an impish look as he intended to convey the message before the actual talking.

'Not now, Dad. I already told you we are all fine. Here is the thing, when we are ready, you and Mom will be the first ones to know, and that is a promise. Happy?' The son was so sincere that the old man couldn't say no. He nodded with a smile and the deal was done. No more talking about children.

'Thanks, Dad! Please enjoy your special tea,' the son said with a sigh of relief and went back to the kitchen where his mom and wife were waiting. As he joined them again, the son and his wife started talking quietly while the mother afforded herself a smile and pretended that she had heard nothing at all.

While dinner was being prepared, the father enjoyed the special tea and watched TV on his own. By the time dinner was ready, it was 7 p.m. and the whole family gathered around the dinner table. The large round wooden dining table with four folding metal chairs was a very simple affair.

For dinner, the women had prepared chicken curry, mixed vegetables, lentils, tomato chutney and fried rice. Ram and his wife were seated on one side and the son and his wife were seated on the opposite side. Unlike Chinese family dinners, where food is normally served from the centre of the table, the meal here was served individually in a special stainless-steel plate that had various pockets for different dishes. It was just the lentils that were served in a separate soup bowl. The old folks from the village would normally eat with their hands but nowadays people use mostly forks and spoons, and not to embarrass themselves in front of a Chinese daughter-in-law, they opted for the spoon and fork.

'Unlike Chinese food, which are mostly steam-cooked, the taste here is totally different, and I just love it,' Teresa declared, showing her new loyalty, and it was not only spoken in order to please her mother-in-law.

'You should come here more often and learn how to cook it so you can have it every day,' Ram enthused as he poured lentils on top of the fried rice.

'That's what I am doing, Father. I actually helped Mother in the kitchen today, right?' she said with a child-like enthusiasm and looked toward the mother for her endorsement.

'Yes, she really did, and I am sure that she will learn everything soon.' Gauri Maya nodded in agreement.

'The chicken curry is so good, and I am going to eat everything tonight without thinking much about gaining weight,' the daughter-in-law said and dug in. She was not only eating fast but also making noises while eating, and it clearly showed that she was relishing the food.

'You know what, dear, they said curry dishes enhance our immune system and people don't get sick that easily,' Ram said with a smile.

'All Hong Kong people were eating curry during the SARS outbreak, remember? The Indian restaurants did very good business during that time,' his son added.

'Oh really! Was it true or just some sort of cunning business scheme, trying to take advantage of people's emotions?' Teresa inquired.

'It was real. A pragmatic bunch, like Hong Kong people, they suddenly started liking curry and Indian dishes.' The son sounded sarcastic but there was truth in his saying.

'Don't you use the same herbs and spices we do in Chinese cooking?' Gauri Maya asked. Since she knew very little about Chinese food, she was naturally curious.

'We do. Actually we have particular sauces for different dishes. But the biggest difference in our cooking is that we use them separately, after cooking, while you put them in together during the cooking. That's why it mixes well and tastes better,' the daughter-in-law explained, and it actually made sense.

'You are absolutely right,' Ram said, appreciating her explanation.

'We also don't chop the vegetables into small pieces as you do here,' Teresa said as she scooped a spoonful of the mixed vegetables for a good chew.

'Try some chutney, it is the most essential part of our cuisine, and we hardly eat without it,' Gaura Maya said and waited until the daughter-in-law had tried it.

'The taste is so strong but fresh. I liked it.' She couldn't stop eating, which made her mother-in-law genuinely happy.

'I don't think you have daal here in Hong Kong. I mean lentil. It is a typical South Asian dish and people have it almost on a daily basis,' Ram said and asked her to have a try. She had already been here a few times before, but each visit turned out to be like a new one, and her reactions made everyone happy. And why wouldn't it? After all, people never tire of talking about their national cuisine, and the Gurung household was no different.

There also was another benefit whenever the daughter-in-law had visited. She loved her mother-in-law's cooking so much that each time she ended up licking her fingers as a small child and that would make Gauri Maya extremely happy. Although everyone would start with a spoon and fork, it was the daughter-in-law who always ended up eating with her hands just like the old Nepalese folks back in the village.

'Mom and Dad, we have something to say to you tonight.' The son waited until dinner was finally over and everyone was about to get up. His words stopped that and made everyone remain seated. He looked at them all in turn and said, 'We want you two to come and stay with us. You have worked enough; our place is big enough for all of us and it is about time that you two take some rest. What do you say?'

It was not only sudden but also a big thing for any proud parents. The father and mother instantly realized the significance of the son's request and got emotional. They didn't know how to react and were speechless for almost a minute. It took quite a while before they could start talking again.

'It is a very happy and proud moment for us,' Ram finally cleared his throat and replied with a firm voice. 'Thanks to both of you, really appreciate it. But we think, your mother and I, it is not the right time for us to move in. Thank God, we are still strong and able, we like this place a lot, and all of our friends are here as well. You are still young. You still have a long way to go before you can have a well-established career and it might not be a good idea that we join in. We know you have been good and responsible to us, and you both want to help us. But there is still time for that, Son, and hope you will understand our position. You have asked, that is already a big thing for us, and let me tell you this, we are really happy and proud. We simply couldn't ask for more. God bless you two, may all of your dreams and wishes come true. Be happy and healthy.'

'We only have you two as our closest family, you are our son and daughter-in-law, and when we become old and weak, of course, we will come knocking on your door,' Gaura Maya said. 'Where else can we go? But as for now, as your father has already said, we are still fine and can stand on our own. We both are still working; whatever we earn is enough for our simple life and you don't have to worry about us for now. Therefore, please don't be hard on yourselves, keep visiting us whenever you have free time, and everything will be just fine. And when the time will finally come, and we are not able to take care of ourselves anymore, we will pack our bags and come straight to your place,' she concluded.

'It will be not only be our pleasure but also our honour to have you two at our place and we are not saying this just for the sake of it,' the daughter-in-law said, and the son had to interpret it before the parents could understand it.

Despite belonging to a completely different race, Teresa had proved her virtue and character, and made them all happy and proud. The old couple knew that their son was in good hands.

Chapter 19

The night was bright and mild; a nice evening for an outing and the place they had chosen was just perfect. It was an outside café with a sea view and relatively less crowded. The stunning Victoria Harbour had fewer boats hence those bright lights beaming from the skyscrapers on the other side were reflecting on the water's surface and creating colours that only added to the beauty of the night.

The big promenade was actually the rooftop of the whole building that happened to be the ferry terminal from where fast boats to China's coastal cities departed. The café occupied a small portion of the promenade. The other parts of the promenade were open to the public and there were still some people walking along it.

The café had ten seats in the open area, each seat had a square table and two chairs made of aluminium with a synthetic rattan seat, and only half of the seating was occupied. On one side, the café had extended to the edge of the promenade, which had a glass railing and the other side was the exterior of the tall building. Everything served on the café was supplied from the indoor kitchen and the outside area was only for seating.

The seat on the right-hand corner facing the harbour had two square tables joined with six chairs on each side. Two seats facing the harbour were occupied by the parents, seated opposite them were the sons-in-law, and both daughters were seated on the right and left, next to their respective husbands. The occasion was a family dinner arranged by the sons-in-law in respect of their in-laws.

'Thank you for accepting our invitation. It means a lot to us and is appreciated,' Adam, the white husband of first daughter Rekha Thapa said politely.

'Same here, thanks, bro!' The second daughter Disha Thapa's black husband, Joe, said briefly in a harsh voice. Both parents grinned.

'What would you like to have for a drink?' Adam asked.

'Beer!' Sher Bikram Thapa wanted to say but instead blurted out, 'Water is fine, thank you!' Gita Thapa also asked for water instead of soda.

'We are thinking of having a light white wine, right dear?' Adam asked for an opinion from his wife before turning towards the other two. 'What would you guys like to have then?'

'Beer for me. What about you?' Joe said without hesitation and asked his wife.

'I will have a cold lemon tea,' Disha Thapa responded indifferently.

Adam raised his hand, and when a woman in a black dress appeared, he ordered the beverages. As everyone waited for their drinks, Adam checked the menu.

It didn't take long for the drinks to arrive.

'So, what would you all like to have for dinner?' Adam politely asked again as he passed the menu around. 'Please don't hesitate. Anything you like, please ask. After all, this is the very first time that we have invited you.'

'Thank you!' Sher Bikram Thapa said as he took the menu and started turning the pages. He was a simple man who hardly frequented such places. He did not recognize any of the dishes on the menu as they had weird names that he had never heard of in his entire life. Gita Thapa's situation was no better, and she had been hoping for him to find a way out for both. He looked uneasily at the menu, then at his wife and awkwardly smiled. Thankfully, the others were busy making their own choices and weren't looking at them.

They pretended as they were busy selecting the items and didn't look up until everyone was ready to order. By then, he had already thought out a plan to avoid unnecessary embarrassment.

'Are you guys ready to order?' Adam asked again and everyone turned to the parents. They were elderly, and it was a mark of respect in Asian society to ask them first.

'We are not very familiar with such food, as you know since we hardly come here. Why don't you just order something for both of us?' Sher Bikram Thapa managed to say somehow and gave back the menu with a sigh of relief.

Every time he saw Adam speak, he thought of the white officers when he was in the army, and couldn't help but remember how they had been beyond reach, and, today, as he shared the same table with a white man, it made him uncomfortable.

The food had finally arrived. Rekha Thapa and her husband had spaghetti with clams, fresh leek, shredded cheese in tomato sauce, fresh salads with Thousand Island dressing, and Chilean white wine. Disha Thapa and her husband had pizza with pepperoni, mushroom and a hamburger with fries. Sher Bikram Thapa and Gita Thapa had ordered mixed grills of chicken, pork, beef and sausage with black pepper sauce, and borsch soup as a starter.

Joe had a few more beers while Adam and his wife finished up a bottle of white wine and the old parents drank more plain water. As they all dug in, they hardly spoke, and only Adam and his wife murmured very quietly.

'Would you care for any desserts or just tea or coffee?' Adam asked.

'English tea, please!' Sher Bikram Thapa replied. After visiting UK once while in the army, he knew English tea was not only famous but also a safe bet.

'Me too!' Gita Thapa followed her husband's lead and grinned.

'I will have a coffee, man, black coffee without milk, just sugar,' Joe said and started picking his teeth using a toothpick from the table. Adam went for English tea while the two daughters decided not to have anything.

'Thank you for the nice meal, it was really good,' Sher Bikram Thapa said out of courtesy and drank the English tea. The tea was as bland as a mixture of hot water, milk and tea. But he drank it anyway and pretended as if he were actually enjoying it.

'Our pleasure and thank you!' Adam sounded happy and Joe acknowledged it with a grunt. The two daughters hardly said anything.

'Since we are already family now, I think we should now try to learn more about each other. So, what is your plan for the coming future?' Sher Bikram Thapa heard himself saying. He could hardly believe what he had just said and wondered how he had suddenly become so daring.

'Well, as for the future plan…!' Adam was lost for words. He certainly didn't expect the reserved old man to ask such a question out of nowhere. The others waited as he tried to regain composure.

'Sorry, if this sounds sudden, but I am a father and I certainly have concerns for my girls. Hope you don't mind.' Sher Bikram Thapa had realized the situation and tried to amend it. Thanks to his long-term association with his other friends, he had learned the skills of engaging in conversation and how to conduct one.

'Please, don't be sorry, you have every right to ask such questions,' Adam said. He had recovered well by then. 'My work is going well, the pay and perks are good and we already have our own place. We also don't have any plans of leaving Hong Kong soon or to start a family. But before that, as this is her dream; he pointed towards Rekha Thapa, we might try to open a beauty parlour of her own, and she can use her skills in the world of beauty without having to worry about anything else. I think it makes sense as she is a beautician herself, and she knows the trade. It will definitely be a very interesting thing for us and as long as she is happy, I am happy.'

'Thank you dear, you are a good man,' Rekha Thapa said and affectionately looked towards Adam, who in return kissed her on the lips as if they were alone. The old couple looked away in embarrassment.

'Thank you so much for taking care of our girl, we are really happy. God bless you,' Sher Bikram Thapa said and Gita Thapa nodded in agreement.

'Appreciated and thank you!' Adam said and held his wife's hand. Now the attention was turned towards Joe and his wife, and everyone waited patiently until they were ready to talk again.

'My business is still new; I need sometime before it can be established and only then can we afford our own place. Sorry to disappoint, we come from a rather different world and have to work harder than others. But we are trying, you know, we are really trying hard, man, and hope things will get better soon. Please don't worry, old man, it will be alright and I can promise you that I will always do my best. Right, honey? Together we will make our life better and try to remain happy. It is a difficult world, but we will work hard. And eventually everything will work out well.' Joe said with a determined look and tried to force a smile.

Life is already hard for a brown man; you are a black man, son, Sher Bikram Thapa said to himself and tried to appear normal from the outside. Just like the whole world, he knew the vast difference between a black and a white man, and the only thing he could do now was hope for the best.

Fate played a tricky game on him. All he had wished for was a normal life for his daughters with Nepali boys as husbands, but what he got were a black man and a white man for sons-in-law. He genuinely didn't know how to react.

'Everything is in our fate. I know you might not believe in such a thing as fate, but for us, fate plays a huge role in our life and what is important is fate, not the face that has to be strong, and only then can life become beautiful. In addition, we don't know what fate has in store for us tomorrow. Therefore, all we can do is try our utmost and hope for the best,' Sher Bikram Thapa said in a solemn voice. Just like all the parents out there, all he wanted was a good and healthy life for his children.

'We just want you to have a happy, healthy and memorable life. What else can a parent ask for? If you are happy, we are happy!' Gita Thapa said.

'We are really happy to see you all tonight. It is very nice of you all, and please don't forget to visit us whenever you have time, okay,' Sher Bikram Thapa said.

'Thank you, and we will,' Adam and Joe replied at once.

'Please take good care of yourselves and have a safe trip back home,' the two daughters said, and held their mother's hand.

The daughters kept waving their hands until the parents were out of sight and headed towards the West Rail line for a trip back home. The Austin Road train station was just a ten-minute walk from the place the parents had dinner, and they decided to walk.

'Thank God, the meeting went well. I was quite nervous!' Sher Bikram Thapa finally said with a sigh of relief.

'I also had the same feeling at the beginning. After all, we were not only meeting foreigners but also two different types. I am really glad that all went well and it is finally over,' Gita Thapa couldn't hide her happiness as well as relief.

'We must certainly be the only Nepalese parents with a white man and a black man as sons-in-law. Isn't that weird?' Sher Bikram Thapa pointed out. No matter how ironic or scathing they sounded, they were just expressing what they felt inside.

'I couldn't even imagine in my wildest dreams that such a thing would happen to us,' Gita Thapa said.

'You are absolutely right. A white man and a black man as sons-in-law, and had it not actually happened to us, we couldn't have ever believed it. People say sons-in-law are like your own son but as far as we are concerned, it is simply not in our luck at all,' Sher Bikram Thapa said as he lamented his fate of not having his own son.

By now they had already arrived at the train station, so they took the escalator down and waited for the train on the underground platform.

'The last train must have just left. The other one is coming within the next three minutes. As rush hour is over, I hope it is not that crowded,' Sher Bikram Thapa said as they waited.

'I am still worried about the youngest one. Don't know what she saw in him. He seemed neither rich nor handsome. It still puzzles me,' Gita Thapa said, grimacing. She wasn't complaining, but trying to reason things out for her own assurance. Doubts are terrible things; they can keep many restless souls awake at night.

'It is karma, I suppose. They were meant for each other and destined to meet there in Hong Kong, what else?' Sher Bikram Thapa found an easy target to blame.

'The white guy seemed to be quite nice and polite. At least he should keep the eldest one happy. One less thing to worry about for both of us, don't you think?' Gita Thapa said optimistically.

'I can understand your feelings but if you ask me, the only thing I see on a white man is the face of an army officer. They used to operate in such a condescending way as if they had come from a totally different planet. They looked and acted as if they were very superior to us Gurkhas. But now it seems that they were just trying to show us we were inferior. Anyway, it still creates an uneasy and awkward situation inside of me, and I can hardly behave in a natural way. That was precisely what bothered me during the meeting, but eventually I felt better, and I think I am fine now,' Sher Bikram Thapa said. He appeared relieved.

Just then the train arrived, and they got in and found seats for themselves.

'The food was good but don't you think that there was still something missing?' Gita Thapa asked as she settled down on the metal seat.

'What do you mean? Don't say you are still hungry,' Sher Bikram Thapa inquired.

'No, no, I am completely full but it still feels like the craving is not satiated yet. It is like you just ate curry and vegetables the whole time, and there was no rice,' Gita Thapa explained.

'Right there, you said it all. Your answer is your own explanation. There was no rice, remember? That's why!' Sher Bikram Thapa proclaimed in a triumphant voice. 'It is like going to the party in tight attire, like I did, and this suit is still making me uncomfortable. With such tight clothes, I can eat the best things in the world and still not be satisfied. I am desperate to take them off. This is all because of our habits. We like new things on one hand, but we are also afraid of adopting them on the other. We need some time before we can accept them.'

'When did you start talking like that? Not bad ha...!' Gita Thapa said with a surprised look.

'I have friends!' Sher Bikram Thapa replied.

'I would certainly want to meet them,' she said in a teasing voice.

'No problem at all,' he replied in a similar tone.

Chapter 20

Dinner was served earlier than usual. Laxmi Sharma had prepared a big and sumptuous dinner for all, and she had cooked at least one favourite dish for each family member. Tonight was a special night for the Sharma household and all the family members had come, including the sons-in-law and children. Dinner was a noisy but lively affair, which lasted for almost two hours, and everyone had the best time of their lives.

After the big dinner, everyone gathered in the living room and earnestly waited for the patriarch to make the special announcement. The men and elderly women sat on the sofa while the children made themselves comfortable on the carpeted floor. The single sofa seat facing the store was reserved for the head of the family, Krishna Sharma, from where he was to make the special announcement very soon.

'Everyone is here, right?' Krishna Sharma cleared his throat and looked around like a proud lion overseeing his ever-expanding herd before speaking. Everyone was instantly alert and waited with bated breath.

'Although I never said it before openly, I am going to say it tonight to all of you. Thank you so much for coming here. I am very happy as well as grateful. As you all know, I have never shied away from talking in life. Perhaps it is in our clan. But talking about eking out a living, and talking from the heart are two completely different things. A man is a liar if he says he doesn't feel nervous when talking from the heart, and my position is no different. But we all have to go through such stages in our lives sooner or later, and we must talk directly from the heart. Tonight is one of those moments for me as well, and I am not finding it any easier if I am to be honest. We have responsibilities; a big man has big responsibilities and small men have small ones, but we all have responsibilities that we must fulfil. It is one of those moments now and a responsible man shouldn't run away from it. My time has come and this is precisely what I am doing now.' Krishna Sharma's voice had taken on a solemn tone by the time he ended his speech. He drank some water before continuing again.

'We come into this world, do our work and eventually leave. People come and go, today's new generation becomes the older generation by tomorrow, and the cycle continues forever. Nobody can stop the course of time; we all have to follow its course and make changes accordingly. I think that time has arrived in your family as well. It is time for new changes and the old generation has to move on to make space for the new one. I have already thought about it in great detail. Please remember that whatever decisions I made were not done in a hurry or because of emotion. My decisions are final. I am not going to change anything and please just respect them.' He said it and drank more water. The family members looked at each other in total astonishment and confusion.

'Bishnu my son, please listen carefully!' Krishna Sharma cleared his throat again and started, 'As the first son of the family, I am handing over the main family business to you and you should take over immediately. You have already been learning this trade for years, you know the business inside out, and you will be fully responsible for running the business on your own henceforth. You will decide what products to buy, where to buy them from and at what price. I will provide advice only when and if you ask for it and will never intervene. It will be entirely up to you how to run it and how to make it a successful business. It is about time that we pass the family torch down to the younger generation, and you have no choice but to carry on with the family legacy. How you want to do it is your own decision, Son, and God bless you!'

'But, Father, how can I do that? The grocery business is like your life; it lives in you. How can I be so cruel to separate it from you?' Bishnu Sharma cried out. Krishna Sharma was not only his father but also a mentor and everything he had learned in life was from him. The son had too much respect for the father and he was hesitating.

'I think you haven't paid much attention to what I have just said,' Krishna Sharma thundered; of course the scolding was tinged with affection for his son. 'This is what I have been trying to explain to you, and I am not going to repeat that again. My decision is final, and you better get a grip on it. I am not asking you to pick up the moon, right?'

'You shouldn't worry too much and just listen to your father, Bishnu,' Laxmi Sharma butted in. The women of the Sharma household hardly spoke while the elders were discussing important things. She was the matriarch and the position came with special privileges.

'Ganga and dear son-in-law, as the first daughter and son-in-law of the family, you will take over the hundi business and run it independently for the family. I am going to introduce all the key players of the business to you right away and explain to you how things are done in this business. All you need is a mobile, a little bit of talking and checking bank transactions on a regular basis. Most importantly, you must learn how to trust the right people and follow your own instincts. Without trust in this business, you are going nowhere, and betrayal means disaster. Hope I have made it all clear and I am sure that you will make a very good businessman. God bless you!' Krishna Sharma then explained the other portion of the family business to the eldest daughter and her husband and paused before drinking more water.

'Thank you so much, Father and Mother, for finding us suitable for such a big honour,' Ramesh said. I can't describe my happiness in words.' He was talking on behalf of his family, and he was genuinely grateful. 'It would not only be my privilege but also an honour to be a part of this great family. I am blessed. I will do whatever you have me do, and will always do my best to make you proud. I will never let you down. All my family and I need is your blessing and as long as it keeps coming, I have no worries in the world. Thank you so much again. I will never disappoint you.'

'Thank you, dear son-in-law, we are really glad that we have you as the life partner of our daughter, and please always remember that we are family,' Krishna Sharma said emotionally. He was genuinely touched by his son-in-law's words.

'We are really lucky indeed to have you, and please always keep that in mind,' Laxmi Sharma pitched in.

'Thank you so much, Father and Mother,' Ganga Sharma, the first daughter said with tears in her eyes.

'Hari, my dear son, as the youngest son of the family, you will inherit this house and you can do whatever you want here. I suppose, since you are a qualified doctor, you can turn it into a private medical clinic and treat patients from the neighbourhood. It is just an opinion, it is up to you, and you can decide as you like. I am going to give you a month's time to think it over and let us know your final decision whenever you are ready. Don't take too much time on it, ha… You are already a grown-up now and you should start taking responsibility soon.' Krishna Sharma's young son had returned from Beijing after the completion of his medical courses, and it was about time he started making plans for the future.

'Yes, Father. Thank you so much. I totally understand,' Hari

Sharma acknowledged softly. He knew he had no escape route, and decided to accept the situation that his father had set up for him.

'In the meantime, you should also settle down soon, and we are going to make the necessary arrangements for you,' Krishna Sharma said. It was as if he had thrown a new bomb that exploded in the room and made everyone move in all directions at once.

'We should start looking for a girl right away,' Laxmi Sharma said in such a euphoric voice that she sounded like a teenage girl.

The room was suddenly transformed, everyone had a smile plastered on their face, and the seriousness of the moment was forgotten for a few moments.

'If you have anything to say, speak out now, otherwise it will be too late,' Bishnu Sharma, the elder brother, said. He couldn't pass over a chance of teasing his younger brother while it was still appropriate and indulged himself with a big laugh. The others agreed and continued pestering the poor guy for a while.

'Now, Radha, dear, it is your turn to listen up!' As Krishna Sharma cleared his throat and started speaking again in a serious voice, everyone suddenly stopped and listened. 'Since you have already finished your studies, it is about time you started thinking about the future, and if you have anything in mind, please let us know. I understand you are from the modern generation and we have differences. But certain things in life remain the same for many generations and they have hardly changed. Right and wrong and the change of time won't affect life that much either. Unless you have a very good reason, it is about time that we start thinking about your future and look for an ideal groom. Of course, we will arrange a meeting with you two when we have found the right one, and you will always have the final say. We will never marry you off without your final acceptance and that is a promise to the princess from her loving parents. And as she is the youngest sister of you all, all the brothers should also pitch in, and help find the best husband for our lovely princess.'

'But, Dad, I just finished my studies, and I am not ready yet,' Radha Sharma complained. She could raise her voice only because she had been pampered as the youngest child, and her shenanigans were forgiven as a tantrum.

'You have already finished university, dear, you are not a small girl anymore, and it is time that you start listening to your old man, alright?' Krishna Sharma said, trying to appear firm and decisive on his position.

'Had we been back in Nepal, you would have already become a mother of three children by now. Please understand!' Laxmi Sharma expressed her opinion.

'Time is of essence, dear, time doesn't wait for anyone, and we must do things at the right time. If not, it will be too late, and again, it will be harder to catch up in life. It is about time dear, and we cannot postpone it anymore. Please listen to your parents. No parents want unpleasant things for their children and we are no exception,' Krishna Sharma explained.

'I just finished university, so I wanted to have some work experiences before being tied down. I don't think it is too much to ask for,' Radha Sharma said, almost in tears. She knew she was losing the battle.

'You can still work after marriage if you insist. It shouldn't be a big deal, right, Father?' Bishnu Sharma pitched in and that somehow settled the ongoing matter.

'Exactly! Who said you cannot work after marriage? This is the modern age; everybody works after marriage and you should also do the same. That's all we will say about this matter, and I will take it that the discussion is closed,' Krishna Sharma said.

'In addition to what I have said tonight, we will still remain a close-knit family and all the businesses will remain as the combined businesses of the Sharma household. Although I will not interfere in running the businesses on a daily basis, you will still present the business report at the end of the month to me, and fifty per cent from the total profit must be handed over to me until further notice. You can call it my share of commission or pension; it doesn't matter and I will not tolerate any dishonesty or cheating whatsoever from any one of you. It might sound harsh now, but it is better to be clear than sorry, and I want you all to take it seriously. At the end of the day, it is my business, and I want to make sure that it survives generation after generation. Hope I have made it all clear, and I genuinely hope that you won't disappoint me. Thank you and that's all for tonight.' Krishna Sharma had made things amply clear. As everyone nodded in agreement, he felt relieved.

His job here was finally done and he was ready to hang up his gloves once and for all.

'Hope you will still be with us here in this house and brighten up our days,' Hari Sharma said, hoping that the parents would say yes.

'No son, we will not be here with you in the future,' Krishna Sharma said in such a mysterious way that it took them by surprise. Everyone wondered what surprises were in store. They didn't have to wait too long. He caressed his moustache and chin gently and continued, 'As we all know, Jordan areas have become almost uninhabitable for decent people.

Thanks to our own people, it has turned into a ghetto, and I don't want to spend my old days here in perpetual danger. We have drug addicts here, our youngsters fight almost every night, each building has an illegal drinking place, our people drink and fight, ignoring our children's future, and there are too many illegal activities taking place here. The good name of our Gurkhas is totally ruined by the new generation, and the last thing I want to do is to raise my grandchildren here. Therefore, we are moving out soon.'

'Where to, Father...? We didn't hear you say!' Hari Sharma asked with a shocked look. The others were in a similar situation and nobody had the slightest clue.

'To Kam Tin, I have worked enough here. We are going to have a village house with front, back and rooftop gardens. I am going to grow flowers as well as vegetables and will live a nice and quiet life. I want to have a change, a nice change where life is slow and peaceful. It is time for us to take rest and that is precisely what we are going to do. It is time for the young ones to work and earn their stripes,' Krishna Sharma said.

'Hari Babu, you will use this place only as your clinic and you will commute from our new place in Kam Tin.'

'We do not want your children to grow up here in such a horrible place,' Laxmi Sharma finished what her husband had started and felt really good about it. The old couple had already discussed it before the meeting.

'And I am going to have a dog of my own as well. That will be just perfect!' Krishna Sharma finally said and already started dreaming of the future. His serious look gradually turned to a happy one.

We are all born with brains, but wisdom comes only with age, and that night's event in the Sharma household was the best example. Krishna Sharma, the family head, had really worked and planned hard for the family and truly deserved the happy ending.

Chapter 21

It was a lazy Sunday morning, the streets below were not as busy and crowded as other working days, and the heat and humidity of the summer was being gradually replaced by the mild and sunny days of late autumn. Unlike other Sunday mornings, all the members of the Biswakarma family had woken up early and were busy in the living room that particular morning and trying to outsmart each other as if it were some sort of race in the making.

The family restaurant, which was situated on the ground floor, normally opened at 4 p.m. and there was plenty of time before the restaurant's opening. It was quite an unusual scene, to say the least. They had gathered in a timely manner for a very special reason. Most surprisingly, it was the children who were working hard in the kitchen while both parents were told strictly to remain seated on the sofa. They decided to cook a special breakfast for their parents and chose an English breakfast for the menu.

After a long and persistent struggle in the kitchen, the new cooks eventually came out winners, and the special breakfast was finally ready to be served. It consisted of a double-yoked pan-fried egg, sweet beans, sliced and fried bacon, English sausage, and toasted bread with butter and jam accompanied by English tea in a decorative teapot with milk and sugar in a separate pot. The China teacup and saucer had a similar decoration as the teapot with a stainless-steel teaspoon. The breakfast was served on a big white China plate in a flowery pattern. The fork, spoon and knife were of stainless steel and spotlessly shiny. Seeing the presentation alone seemed like they had worked extremely hard. What was presented on the table was really good, and the parents could not have asked for more.

'Before you start, please, Mom and Dad, we would like to say a few words,' Michael BK implored with a smile as he stood in front of the parents. Donna BK, who was still tidying up the kitchen, joined him at the side. 'Since you have been taking care of us until now, we both wanted to do something special for you to demonstrate our sincere gratitude, and this meal was what we decided was the best. Hope you like it, please accept our small gesture and start now.'

'This is our very small way of saying thank you, hope it tastes good and you will like it,' Donna BK said with a smile.

'I am sure it will taste just great. After all, you have put so much love and effort into it,' Manohar BK said with a proud smile and grabbed a fork and a knife.

'I couldn't agree more. I am really excited to give it a try. Can we eat now?' Parvati BK asked with sparking eyes. She couldn't wait to dig in.

'Please go ahead!' Michael BK said.

'Wow! It's really good,' Parvati BK said as she took the first bite and started chewing it as if it were the best dish she had ever eaten in life.

'I am really surprised that you two can make such a nice breakfast,' Manohar BK said, echoing his wife's words. Then he started tasting each item from the plate without stopping.

'Really good! I can't believe it! Delicious!' Parvati BK said with her mouth full. She could hardly pronounce the words correctly, there was so much food in her mouth.

'Oh, really! Was it really that good?' Donna BK covered her face with both hands and exclaimed.

'Are you sure? Hope you are not saying this just to make us happy. Please be honest, ha..., you know we are grown-up now and can take the criticism. You don't have to pretend anymore. Okay, Mom and Dad!' Michael BK said sceptically, as he was clearly having some doubts about his parents' remarks.

'Why should I lie? It is truly amazing and I really like it,' Manohar BK replied immediately and his sincere face showed no inkling of insincerity or pretence.

'Exactly! I know we are biased as parents sometimes but this is just great. And believe me, I don't even have to wear that particular hat now and that is a good thing, as a matter of fact. Really!' Parvati BK explained with twinkling eyes. Joy was plastered all over her face.

'Hmmm…, that is really great. You know how scared we were. Now I can sigh with relief and thank God, you liked it,' Donna BK said enthusiastically. She seemed relieved.

'Yes, sister! I am really happy that it went as planned. It felt just great!' Michael BK said while looking at his sister. 'Give me a high five, sister!' He raised his right hand and got a nice slamming from his over-excited sister in return.

'Great job, we are really proud of you two,' Manohar BK congratulated them.

'Yes, really great job. Congratulations! Why don't you join us then?' Parvati BK asked.

'I am sure that you must also be hungry by now!' Manohar BK added.

'Good idea. I had almost forgotten about it. Thanks for reminding us,' Michael BK said sat down to eat.

'You are right, brother. Suddenly I am hungry,' Donna BK said and sat next to her brother. They didn't talk much for a while and enjoyed the breakfast together as they had not done in a very long time.

After finishing the breakfast, they all sat at the dining table and enjoyed the English tea like English aristocrats in the countryside.

'We should do this on a regular basis. I am a fan now,' Manohar BK said as he sipped the tea and put the cup back on the table.

'I totally agree,' Michael BK chimed in.

'Me too! I think it is a good idea,' Donna BK added.

'We just have to cook different dishes next time,' Michael BK suggested.

'It doesn't matter what and who cooks it, what matters is the time we spend together as a family and that should be a reason for us to carry on,' Manohar BK said.

'We run a restaurant for a living and cooking shouldn't be a problem at all,' Parvati BK finally pitched in.

'On a serious note, it also is the perfect time to discuss family matters and make necessary decisions as required by the situation. What do you say?' Manohar BK asked with an impish look on his face, which suggested he had something on his mind.

'Why not? I think family matters are good to be discussed in great detail before making any decision and this should be the right time,' Michael BK agreed.

The two ladies of the house nodded in agreement but didn't say anything.

'We have been thinking about it a lot lately,' Manohar BK said as he cleared his throat, looked intently towards his wife and started again with a firm voice. 'Time doesn't wait for anyone and we are not going to be any younger either. It has been a while since you finished your studies and it is about time we started talking about your future. As the first son of our family, you have certain responsibilities towards your family and we should start discussing them before it is too late. So, what do you say? Have you thought of any plans for the future?'

'I know what you mean, Dad, I really do,' Michael BK said without flinching. He seemed to know it was coming and was well prepared. 'I also happen to have similar thoughts lately and wanted to have a talk about it. I was actually talking about the same issue with Donna just a few days ago and perhaps it is the right time for a change.'

'Yes, Dad and Mom, we also wanted to discuss some issues and are glad that you have brought up the subject at the right time,' Donna BK pitched in. The siblings seemed well prepared, which would make the discussion easier for all.

'I am really happy to hear that. You two are really grown-ups by now.' Parvati BK couldn't hide her joy.

'That's really great news! We are here to listen and provide our best advice,' Manohar BK said as a proud parent. He was ready and excited to hear it out.

'My desire and passion of serving the public is over for good,' Michael BK said, before restarting. 'I thought that if I was honest, passionate and happy, I could make changes in society, and I really believed it. But society is not that simple. Humans are probably the most complicated creatures, and we need plenty of exposure as well as experience to understand them. There are many aspects of our life that could stop us from moving ahead and many things cannot be taken for granted. If we have our ego, pride, status and class on the one hand, we have envy, greed, desire and thirst for power on the other. Finding a balancing act between them is a very difficult task. Especially in a society where people are less privileged, and self-enriching is the norm of the day. Life can be pretty rough and achieving middle ground is almost impossible. Sometimes nothing concrete can be achieved by any means and all we do is talk.'

'That is what I have been saying from the very beginning,' Manohar BK butted in. 'Especially in a society like ours, nothing can be done. Our society is probably the most divided one. First there is caste, sub-caste, then region, village, and clan, etc. We have our own different groups; one won't help or join the others, and see each other as rivals. We can never become one with unity: lack of it is our main problem. In addition, we have political factions and we play party politics even here in Hong Kong as we used to fight back in Nepal. We have more organizations than people here in Hong Kong, and everyone wants a chair. We want power without responsibility. Our so-called community leaders have no skill, experience or knowledge to lead, all they want is the chair and to do nothing in return to help support the community. In fact, our entire community has become so selfish and short-sighted that nobody budges without personal gain. What can you expect from such a dysfunctional society and the earlier we abandon it, the better it is, Son.'

'I have already realized that by now, Dad. I am already done with that phase of my life and decided to move on. Like you said, I think it is about time I started helping you at the restaurant and share the responsibility. I will start working there right away and learn all the tasks from the basics so I can take over when you are ready to take a step back, and then I will carry on with our family business. I think it is the right thing to do, and I will work hard to make sure that you are not disappointed. Please let me know if this is okay with you. I am ready to accept whatever decision you take in the end. Please just let me know.' After Michael BK explained his plan, he waited for his father's final decision.

'Of course it is okay. I cannot even express in words how

happy I am and really pleased that you have thought it all out. That is undoubtedly the best decision we could ever make together, and we have been waiting for so long to hear that. You made the right decision, my son, let's work on it together and I am sure that we will make a great team,' Manohar BK said and it was clear that he was very happy.

'We are really happy and proud of you, Son. Yes, this is the right decision for our family and we should start the good job right away,' Parvati BK pitched in.

'I couldn't agree more. Instead of hiring an outsider, we should work within the family,' Donna BK said, making it obvious that she did not want to be left behind in giving an opinion.

'Now it is your turn, dear.' Donna BK was now the target and squirmed as she found herself on the hot seat. She pretended to be annoyed as her father said, 'Do you have any thoughts about your future? As your studies are over, it is about time you think about it as well.'

'I knew you were going to say that anyway.' She knew his questions were coming and had been preparing herself from within.

'Your father is absolutely right,' Parvati BK commented. She supported her husband as always. 'There is always a right time for everything in our life and you should start preparing for it well before it is too late.'

'I know, I know.' Donna BK said in exasperation. Being the youngest child of the family comes with special benefits. 'It seems like there is no escaping today. I have just finished university and as I wanted to have some work experience before settling down, I applied for an assistant reporter's post at the local English newspaper. I got the job and start this Monday. I didn't say it before as I wanted to give you a nice surprise and hope that you like it now.'

'That's really great, dear. I am really happy for you, congratulations!' Manohar BK beamed with joy. So did Parvati BK and Michael BK. They all congratulated her and wished her a great start.

'Okay, so where were we? Oh, the settling down. I think we should still discuss the prospect of you getting married soon and finally settling down,' Manohar BK told Donna.

'As per our tradition, the older one's turn comes first and it will be you, Michael, about whom we should start talking,' Parvati BK said, reminding everyone of the house rules that most families like her would follow strictly. They weren't ready to break them yet.

Manohar BK continued, 'Your mother is completely right! Let's give priority to you first and then we will concentrate on Donna. If you have anything to say, please say it now, and I can fully guarantee you that we won't make any decision in a rush. We will check all the available options, put them on the table, and give everyone enough time and opportunity to put their points forward. We might be from an old and traditional background, but we fully understand the significance of marriage, and marriage is definitely not child's play. It is the institution that lasts a lifetime; both sides have to be happy and willing before fully committing to holy matrimony. Most importantly, a marriage is not only the unity of two persons but also their whole families, and it is the reason why it has to be accepted by both the families involved. It also cannot happen in a hurry, every possible aspect as well as foreseeable problems have to be anticipated and sorted out before the actual marriage. Therefore, we are not going to impose our decision upon you. We will provide options as well as advice, and the final decision will always be yours. All we want is that you two have a happy, loving and prosperous married life.'

'I fully understand your point, Dad and Mom. I also know that it is for our own good, so thank you very much. We know that you understand our position. I cannot talk on her behalf, but as far as I am concerned, I am perfectly okay with whatever you have arranged for me. You have seen this world, know a thousand times more than me about people, society and even mankind, and I know your choice will be much better than my own. We are probably two of the luckiest children of this world who have such loving and understanding parents like you, and we are really proud and honoured to have you. I think I have already said enough and I should stop and let my sister say something now.'

'Michael has already said it all, and I am totally in agreement with him,' Donna BK said. 'I have nothing to say, and I am perfectly fine with whatever arrangements you would have made or thought about for me. I don't want to repeat the same thing, but like Michael has already said it, your choice will definitely be a lot better than mine, and that is already more than good enough for me. Having said that, I still want you guys to give me some time before settling down so that I can see and experience the world while working and learn from it. Other than that, I just wanted to say how lucky and grateful I am to have you as parents and I love you so much.'

'Oh, that is so sweet of you two. It is not only you but also us who are so lucky to have you two as our children and we couldn't thank God enough. Love you so much!' Parvati BK said, almost crying as she leaned forward to hug them both.

'We are really happy and grateful that we have you two as our children. Thank you and love you so much. Please always remain happy and God bless you!' Manohar BK couldn't hide his emotions, got up from his seat and hugged them all.

Chapter 22

'Emergency! If you don't want to see your loved ones in a sorry situation, come to the address below before 6 p.m. No excuses!'

The first one to receive such a weird text message was Ram Bahadur Gurung, who had just come out of the shower and was preparing himself for his night duty. The next one was Krishna Sharma, who had just returned home from a walk in his new neighbourhood with his newly acquired dog. Then it was Sher Bikram Thapa, who was enjoying the day off, resting in the living room. Manohar BK was about to leave home for the restaurant when he was alerted by the suspicious message. The text message was sent out all at the same time from an unknown mobile and the recipients received it in that particular order.

The suspicious message startled them. They couldn't make sense of it initially, and the uncertainty made them nervous. Especially when family members were alleged to be in danger. They panicked and grabbing their usual gear, they locked the house and headed towards the destination mentioned in the message right away. Amidst the confusion, they did not realize that when they had received the text message, they were alone at home and, surprisingly, all their family members were away. Was it a premeditated plan?

After alighting at Hung Hom train station, it was a ten-minute walk along the road before arriving at an old building at Baker Street, and the designated address was on the second floor of that same old building. When all four friends finally arrived in the interval of just a few minutes, they were totally shocked seeing each other, and it took them sometime before they could start talking about the situation at hand. It was only after they had finished exchanging their surprise that they came to realize that they had been tricked and someone had intentionally brought them together for a reason.

The corridor on the second floor was empty, all the doors were shut, and there was hardly anyone on the entire floor. The door they were supposed to knock on belonged to Flat No. 1, which happened to be just in front of the staircase. The four friends stood still in front of that particular door, and looked at each other. Manohar BK eventually pressed the doorbell. There were some movements inside, and the mysterious door finally opened with a creaking sound.

Before they could go inside, they were greeted with shouts. It was some sort of surprise party or something. 'Surprise! Surprise!' People shouted, whistled and blew party horns. The noise was deafening. The men were taken aback and did not know how to react. They were speechless and it took a while before they could say something. The surprise was carried out in such a discrete yet grand way that it totally took them off-guard. Thank God they didn't pass out.

Slowly the four men realized that the crowd inside the room comprised the four men's family members, friends and other relatives.

Before they could recover and say anything, they were ushered into an artificial gate made by colourful flowers and greeted by four young girls in traditional dresses. The girls offered the men four garlands and yellow scarves that carried religious blessings.

They cut some red ribbon, and the whole room applauded. The new place was officially open and yet the four men had no clue what this place was all about.

'Sorry, uncles, for bringing you all here in such an audacious way, but what could we have done? We all wanted to give you a huge surprise and it just had to start with a bang. I am sure that you will understand our position. If you still want to punish us, fine, please go ahead. But it has to be not only one, two or three, you have to punish each and every one of us here as we all played a part in formulating the plan.' It was Bishnu Sharma, the first son of Krishna Sharma, who started the announcement and everybody listened to him. 'Please keep in mind that we did it because we really love you very much. We did it all for you. At the same time, we also wanted to make it not only special but also memorable, and I am sure we have succeeded in that with flying colours. Do you all agree? If so, please let me have a big round of applause here again and just remember that we really rock, alright!' The whole place was filled with the noise of people clapping furiously.

'Now, please come to this side,' Michael BK, the son of Manohar BK, said. He took over from his elder brother and acted like a new piece of the jigsaw puzzle. He walked behind the bar counter and stopped there until the crowd followed him. 'This is our mini bar. Here you can have all types of drinks, including beer, wine, whiskey, gin, brandy, local ale, soda, tea, coffee, lemon water, etc. It will not only remain open all the time but also is a self-serving one, and you can take any drink you like at any time. What's more, you don't even have to register it. Isn't that just great? Now, ladies and gentlemen, allow me to serve you your first drink tonight. Please come and take whatever drink you want to have. If you are not sure, please allow me to help, thank you!'

Needless to say, the four main guests were the first ones to be served, and the crowd followed suit. Everyone had put on their best clothes for the occasion. It was a colourful mix of people and they looked just fabulous.

'Now, please excuse us and let's move to the next room,' Hari Sharma, the youngest son of Krishna Sharma, said as he led the entire group to the next room. 'Here is our pool table, brand new, and you can play one, two or even four players at a time. The rule is very simple, just put the balls in the hole according to the number and the first one who manages that is the winner. But you will need a lot of practice before being able to hit the ball properly, and a skilful player can do that in a single go. It is also very good for bonding with a friend, relaxing after a long day, and all in all, just for the sake of entertainment as well. I am sure that you will like it very well. If anyone wants to have a try, please come forward.' Everyone looked at each other for a while but nobody came forward for a try. Perhaps it was too unfamiliar for all of them or they were just being modest.

'Let's move to the next room, shall we?' It was Trimol Gurung, the son of Ram Bahadur Gurung who took over from Hari Sharma. 'It is the entertainment room and here we can watch TV, movies and even sing Karaoke.' It had a big flat-screen TV in the front with a set of sofas where at least eight to ten people could easily be seated. 'Here is a list of Chinese, English and Nepalese movies that you can choose from for your entertainment and these are CDs for songs as well as Karaoke. If you have your own choice of song, movie and Karaoke, you can bring them along with you and use them here. It is good for a family gathering, a children's party and other functions, and people from our community can book it for private use. For now, I am going to present a comedy by the local duo in Kathmandu, and we all can have a hearty laugh.' Everyone waited until he was done and suddenly two middle-aged men dressed in typical Nepalese attire appeared on the screen. Sudden spurts of laughter could be heard in the room. The group waited for a while before moving.

Now it was the turn of Rekha, Sher Bikram Thapa's elder daughter. 'Here we can hold family gatherings, children's birthday parties and other small functions from time to time. The room is quite big: in one corner we can prepare the food and beverages, and use the table and chairs to seat people during parties. In the other corner we can have other activities or simply use it for a seating and resting area. Children can sit, play and even draw here, whereas adults can use this place to exercise, do yoga or even meditate. I am sure it will be quite popular for all.' The group looked around but didn't say anything.

'This is the seating place,' said Donna BK, Manohar BK's daughter, who was leading the pack now and explained her part as required. The room was simple, and she said, 'As you can see, it has nothing but just sofas to seat people and side lamps. One can come and rest or remain seated for as long as they like. You can also have a chatting session here, discuss business or family matters in great privacy and have a good time all at the same time. Or you can just come here to get away from the hustle and bustle of a crowded place like Hong Kong, and that is already a bonus for all.' Some of the elders in the group actually sat on the sofas as suggested.

By this time the men had arrived at the last section of the apartment, and the introduction of the new place was about to end. This section had two doors, the first one led to the kitchen while the second opened into a general washroom.

Since the familiarization of the new place was finally over, all those present walked back to the front of the apartment, and everyone went for a refill at the mini bar. The four friends thought that they had probably been invited to facilitate the opening of the new place. Most importantly, nothing had happened as they had feared initially. Everything was fine and none of their families were in trouble. Now they could finally relax and maybe have some nice drink as well, and then return home.

As the four friends sat together, they heard a commotion. 'Excuse me! Excuse me!! Can I have your attention please?' It was Bishnu Sharma again who came forward and tried to gather everyone's attention. Everyone looked at him, including the four friends and they found that he was still in the same lively and mischievous mood as he was at the beginning. They instantly knew that he was up to something.

'The moment has finally arrived, please follow me and help support us to make today one of the special days of our lives.' He started to walk towards a door and the others tacitly followed him. The four old men became really curious because they didn't know what was coming next, but they remained seated.

'Honorary guests, please come this way!' Bishnu Sharma requested the four men as he saw that they had remained seated. Everyone waited until they joined the team. Then they trooped out of the room and gathered outside the door. The four men were standing in front of the crowd and the others crowded around them. Then, Adam and Joe of Sher Bikram Thapa's family, who happened to be the tallest of everyone in the crowd, came forward and stood on each side of the door, facing the crowd. Finally, the moment of truth seemed to have arrived. Adam and Joe turned away and slowly removed the cover from a plaque that was placed right above the main door. A new and shiny name plate appeared on the front that had three words written on it in big white letters against a dark blue background.

THE NAMASTE CLUB

When the four friends finally saw it, they couldn't believe their eyes and instantly realized what was happening. Ram Bahadur Gurung's jaw dropped, Sher Bikram Thapa forgot to blink, Manohar BK held his face with both hands, and Krishna Sharma repeatedly shook his head. Then everybody started clapping. It was a beautiful moment. Emotions ran high, the four men hugged and kissed each other and appreciated the love of their loved ones. It was indeed a very good surprise.

'So it was all about that, ha…!' Krishna Sharma finally managed to speak, all the while staring intently at each of his family members. But it was out of affection, and not anger.

'How did you find out about our secret place?' Ram Bahadur Gurung asked.

'Of course, we knew!' Everyone shouted back in chorus and that surprised the four friends to the core. How could that be possible? They wondered.

'You met there on the last Saturday of each month, made your favourite dish, and ate and drank until very late before returning home. Most importantly, you all talked about all the issues of your life and found solutions accordingly as a unit. We all know everything about it,' Michael BK said with an impish smile.

'But how did you find out? I really want to know, honestly!' Sher Bikram Thapa asked.

'It doesn't matter how we found out, Uncle. What matters is how your four friends are going to enjoy it here. Did we tell you that this whole place was made for you? It is all yours and you can come here anytime you like and you don't have to hide it from your families and friends as well,' Hari Sharma explained and everyone agreed.

'So each and every one of you had a part to play in this and we had no clue, ha..., that is quite impressive, I must say,' Manohar BK said in a disbelieving tone.

'Yes, each and every one of us has contributed to this very special project, and we are really proud of what we have done here,' Bishnu Sharma said with a happy face. 'After we had found out that the original place had been destroyed by fire, we decided to do something about it and worked together to make it a reality. This is your new place, this is 'The Namaste Club' and its door will remain open for as long as you four want. This is our special gift to our loving fathers, and we sincerely do hope that you will like it. Please accept it as a token of our love, care and respect from your dearest families and bless us with eternal joy, compassion and honour. As you know, it was the very first time we came together as a team and were able to do something for you and your acceptance of our present will be one of the happiest moments of our lives. You have done so much for us all, this is nothing in return for what you have done for us, and we still do hope and pray that you will accept it and make our lives meaningful. Please bless us and accept our small gift.'

'It is undoubtedly the most beautiful gift I have ever received in life. I have no words to describe how happy I am and…' Ram Bahadur Gurung couldn't continue.

'It is beyond my imagination. It is definitely the nicest

thing that ever happened to me, I am flabbergasted…!' said an emotional Krishna Sharma.

'I am still finding it extremely hard to ask if this is a dream or reality. So surreal and incomprehensible, somebody please pinch me…!' Sher Bikram Thapa wasn't sure what he had just said and looked around.

'This is just incredible! I still can't believe it is actually happening in front of us, and I genuinely don't know how to express my feelings as well as gratitude,' Manohar BK murmured and started examining the whole place, as he didn't want to miss anything.

'Thank you so much, Uncles and we are really happy that you like it,' Michael BK said on behalf of all the people gathered there and everyone nodded in agreement.

'What a nice surprise! Mind-blowing, don't you think?' Sher Bikram Thapa couldn't hide his excitement.

Everyone hugged each other and it was a beautiful moment, shared and enjoyed by the families. As the special celebration forged ahead in full swing, confetti flew, champagne bottles were unscrewed, music played in full swing, drinks flowed, and food was served non-stop. Everyone was happy, excited and enjoying the party. In no time, the place morphed into one of the happiest places on earth.

Welcome to the newly opened Nepalese club, The Namaste Club.

The party went on until very late at night. Everybody had a really great time, especially the four friends. Despite being on cloud nine, they must have come out and stared gob-smacked at the signboard for at least a dozen times during the night. They never seemed to get tired of seeing it.

The Namaste Club was undoubtedly the most precious gift

they had been given and it remained that way for the rest of their lives. You could take the four men out of the Namaste Club, but you could never take the Namaste Club out of them. They loved and treasured it even more than their own lives. If they had the means, they would have taken the Namaste Club with them to their graves.

Acknowledgements

I always write for a reason, and this book is no exception. Sometimes, the same reason also becomes an obligation, but I have learned never to take it as a burden over time. Writing about my fellow countrymen living in Hong Kong was indeed an honour. I sincerely do hope that I have done a decent job, and please take it as just a mere coincidence if there is any similarity between my story and that of actual people and their lives.

I want to offer my sincere gratitude to the people without whose support the book wouldn't have been possible. My late in-house editor, Victoria Giraud (who passed away recently), Anuj Bahri and the Red Ink Literary Agency team, Tara India Research Press, editor Bidisha Srivastava and the very talented designer of the beautiful cover.

I also want to thank my wife Tina, my son and daughter, and my readers. Without your continuous and unwavering support, I would never have been here, and I am grateful to you all.

TIM GURUNG is a Nepali writer, an ex-Gurkha, and author of the acclaimed Gurkha book, *Ayo Gorkhali*, and lives in Hong Kong with his family.